Nights of the Round Table: Arthurian Erotica
edited by Jennifer Levine

Circlet Press, Inc.
Cambridge, MA

Nights of the Round Table: Arthurian Erotica
edited by Jennifer Levine

Copyright © 2015 Circlet Press, Inc.
Cover copyright © Captblack76 | Dreamstime

Printed in the United States.
ISBN: 978-1-61390-155-7

Print-on-demand edition.

For catalog, information about our imprints, review copies, and other information, please write to:

Published by:
Circlet Press, Inc.
39 Hurlbut Street
Cambridge, MA 02138

Or visit us online at: http://www.circlet.com

Contents

Introduction

King Arthur. Guinevere. Uther Pendragon. Morgana le Fay. Merlin. Sir Lancelot. Sir Gawain. Mordred. Maybe you know all of these names and more; maybe you've only heard of a few. Maybe you've heard of sordid love affairs between some of these characters, or magic enchantments gone wrong, or murders and betrayals among even the closest of friends.

So many stories have already been written about the world of Camelot, and so many remain to be told. For this anthology, we asked writers for both reimagined classics and new tales; dalliances we were expecting and affairs we wouldn't have imagined; familiar characters, new characters, or maybe some we thought we knew but discovered anew in the telling.

In "Wonderly Wroth," Yolande Kleinn explores a world with a cast of characters that are familiar yet nonetheless altogether altered. Merlin is here, but the famed wizard is a woman. Lancelot is as heroic as ever, but here he is somber, aging. Arthur is struck down by Mordred, but he does not die.

In "Destiny" by Katya Harris we see a softer side of Mordred. He rides toward battle, where he knows he must defeat Arthur Pendragon, but he rages at the unfairness of a destiny he did not choose and does not want. When he meets a woman along the way, he begins to imagine a different sort of life, the kind he knows he cannot have.

Jean Roberta takes us back to where it all began, with Igraine and Uther, in "Under the Sign of the Dragon." Igraine finds herself trapped between her husband and King Uther, only one of whom she is in love with. When her husband declares war upon Camelot, Uther resorts to using Merlin's magic to get close to her.

In "Questing," Charles Payseur transports us to modern times, where Lancelot runs through the streets of Chicago. Eternity is a series of quests and games for the immortal Knights of the Round Table, but the one mystery Lancelot has never been able to solve is Palomides, one of his fellow Knights.

"The Giving Game" retells the classic story of the Green Knight, who engages Sir Gawain in a game of generosity. But in Alexandra Erin's version, the nature of this reciprocity may prove to be Gawain's undoing when he finds himself yearning for both the Lady and the Lord of the castle Bertilak.

Finally, Michael M. Jones's "The Shape of Camelot Today" begins with a first date between two (seemingly) ordinary modern women. The catch: Lana, the latest reincarnation of The Lady of the Lake, has a Sword in the Stone sitting in her living room that manipulates her into finding the current reincarnation of Arthur. And Lana is determined to prove that The Once and Future King doesn't have to be a man.

I hope you'll enjoy seeing these legends come to life anew in this anthology. I know I have.

Jennifer Levine
October 2015

Wonderly Wroth
Yolande Kleinn

Even before the blade pierces his armor, Arthur knows that he is meant to die here.

Kings die on battlefields; it's a fate Arthur Pendragon has always accepted. But this is an even greater certainty. He knew before the sun rose that his death waited on this hillside. He's dreamed this battlefield too many times, and then last night, a new dream. His favorite cousin came to him in sleep, though Gawain has been dead since they were both children. He stood in Arthur's tent, small and somber and dressed in his burial robes, and warned Arthur to turn back.

Arthur couldn't turn back, any more than he could send his men into battle without him.

He doesn't repent his decision, even as he feels the bite of steel in his shoulder, piercing through a gap in his mail. Futile rage flashes through him. Mordred is a thug, a stranger intent on carving himself a piece of Arthur's kingdom. He won't succeed—Arthur's knights will see to that—but Camelot will still fall to chaos in Arthur's absence. There is no queen to rule in his stead. Arthur has no children, legitimate or otherwise, and no heirs but for a horde of squabbling cousins to the north. The succession will be fraught, and this one thing he regrets.

The wound cuts deep, and Arthur falls to his knees. He twists painfully to see Mordred standing above him, blade poised for a second fatal blow. Arthur's own sword is in the dirt, and his injured arm hangs useless at his side. He makes no move to escape the inevitable.

A scream of fury pierces the fading clatter of battle, and then a blur of motion and flashing steel cuts Mordred down. Mordred falls, his sword tumbling to the muddy ground. The life fades with surprising swiftness from his eyes.

Arthur stares. His own blood is still rushing out of him with every heartbeat, but he raises his eyes to find Bedivere kneeling beside him. Bedivere's armor is chafed and scored, spattered with blood. His dark eyes are wide with fear, and Arthur offers a smile he doesn't feel.

The fighting has all but stopped around them, and Arthur knows that his army has won. The field is theirs.

Bedivere scans the stilling battlefield, and after a moment he calls out in a ragged voice. "Merlin. Here!"

Arthur blinks, struggling to focus through his blurring vision. He is slumped against Bedivere now, though he doesn't remember losing his balance. Merlin arrives in a swirl of robes and skirts. She kneels at Arthur's side, her ancient face drawn stiff. Her hair, white and thick and tied back from her rigid face, is as blood-spattered as Bedivere's armor, and there is gore smudged across one dark cheek.

There's no hint of fear in Merlin's voice when she turns to Bedivere and commands, "Find Lancelot. Now." They shift Arthur's weight between them, and Merlin's hands are gentle as she settles him carefully to the ground.

"It's all right," Arthur says, though the words sound sluggish on his tongue. "This is how it's meant to end."

"Perhaps." Merlin brushes dark bangs from Arthur's sweat-soaked forehead. "But when have you ever known me to abide by the rules of others?"

Arthur tries to protest, but the last of his strength fails him. A thick fog swallows his senses, dragging him into nothingness and leaving the battlefield at Camlann far behind.

Arthur doesn't wake. Darkness weighs him down too heavily, bearing him away from distant sensations of pain and surrender. The nothingness has faded, but it hovers at the edges of Arthur's jumbled awareness like a patient threat.

Memory jars through him, startling and severe. He sees his throne room awash in sunlight, draped with endless banners of gold and crimson.

His coronation day.

Arthur was twenty-two the day he claimed his father's throne, though by then he'd already been ruling Camelot for three years. He had watched his father's health fail with closing dread, and had taken up a king's responsibilities one by one.

Eventually, only the crown itself remained. When his father died, Arthur took that up too.

Fresh pain cuts through the too-vivid memory, a rising rush of shadows that carry the nothingness forward with it. There's an undercurrent of voices just out of reach, but Arthur can't decipher them. They sound muffled and wrong, distorted by distance. Or perhaps the problem isn't that the voices are too far away, but that Arthur can't listen past the burning pain of his shoulder and the vicious ache beneath his skin.

When the pain fades, the voices fade with it.

He remembers his father in a new, painful flash. Uther Pendragon was a powerful man, stubborn and fearless. His reputation bordered on the mythic by the time sickness took him, making it all the more devastating to watch him die by slow, agonizing degrees. Uther's intimidating height and powerful frame were no match for an illness that even Merlin could not remedy. Her magic bought the dying king more time, and for that Arthur would always be grateful. But she couldn't unmake a mortal disease.

Even magic had limits.

A second surge of pain bursts alight in Arthur's shoulder, though it isn't half so fierce as before. This time when the darkness comes, Arthur is *sure* he hears voices—one voice at least—Merlin murmuring quiet, steady words that he can't make out. His head is too fuzzy to be sure if the problem lies with him or if Merlin is speaking a language he doesn't recognize. Merlin knows half a hundred languages, and not all of them are human.

There's a fire popping and roaring nearby, audible even

through the murk of Arthur's tenuous awareness. He wonders if it's his own hearth—if he's in his own bed—or if his dying soul only desperately wishes it were so.

When the darkness next retreats before memory, Arthur sees Camelot spread beneath him, a familiar view from the eastern parapet. His hands curled tightly over the stone edge.

The year following Uther's death was difficult. Skirmishes on every border signaled a deliberate testing of the new king's mettle, and for a time Arthur despaired of ever restoring peace to Camelot. He fought and negotiated, drew treaties that rarely held his enemies at bay. Those who knew the father always seemed disappointed on meeting the son. Arthur was not so tall as Uther had been. His shoulders were not as broad, his stature not half so imposing as that of Uther Pendragon.

A lean man of unimpressive height, Arthur would have stood unnoticed as a knight. As a king it seemed he was doomed to disappoint.

But Arthur was a man of stubborn character. He may not have shared Uther's intimidating figure, but he had something better: his father's force of will. By Arthur's twenty-sixth birthday, Camelot's borders were as secure as they had ever been during Uther's reign. Treaties were respected, alliances were held sacred.

The surrounding kingdoms learned better manners, and no one dared to cross Camelot's new king.

The encroaching darkness carries only a dull wash of pain this time when Arthur falls from his memories. He hears the heavy thud of a door falling shut, and then Merlin's voice once more. She isn't chanting this time, but she is murmuring too quietly for Arthur to make out the words. For the first time Arthur's curiosity makes him desperate to open his eyes, to see who she's talking to. But struggle as he might against the weight of exhaustion, he only sinks deeper into shadow.

Before he slips too far, he hears a stern, familiar voice ask, "But will he live?" and there is only one face to which un-summoned memory can take him then.

Lancelot of the Lake served Uther Pendragon for years, but it was to Arthur that he gave his fiercest loyalty. The young prince had been only a small child when Lancelot was knighted, but even now Arthur remembers the ceremony with a vivid rush. Lancelot was a young man then. Only seventeen, nobility in search of some greater destiny than growing up a third son in a family who did not need him. He wore brightly polished armor, his sword newly forged for the occasion. He swore himself not only to Uther but to the entire Pendragon line, and Arthur does not remember a Camelot without him.

A fleeting blur passes across the clear memory in Arthur's mind, and in the span of a heartbeat he is looking at a different Lancelot. Older, stronger, his handsome face not the least bit diminished by the passage of years.

Lancelot was a hero in the truest sense, and Arthur admired and adored him for it. By the time Arthur had begun to pay particular notice to the faces at court, Sir Lancelot of the Lake was the most coveted knight in Camelot. There was something intensely somber about him, the weight of responsibility focused and honed like a weapon. His quiet confidence made him distracting, and Arthur Pendragon could ill afford distraction.

Though he spent countless idle fantasies on the idea of Lancelot in his bed, he never once spoke a word to give himself away. He pursued other interests—other men—and never troubled Lancelot with any hint of his fascination.

Arthur had learned the value of secrets long before he became a king.

When true awareness returns, Arthur can no longer escape the unlikely fact that he is not dead. He wakes to sullen daylight skulking through the narrow windows of his chambers. Stone walls and tapestries surround him, and the familiar softness of his own bed. There's a noisy fire in the hearth, and the chamber door stands barely ajar.

Arthur's final memories of the battlefield are clear enough. He moves now with ginger caution and is startled to feel only a dull ache in his shoulder. The wound that should have killed him seems all but healed, and Arthur knows that isn't possible. Merlin's magic is potent, but she can't perform miracles.

Arthur should be dead. He can't fathom why he isn't.

He stares at the ceiling in silence, focusing on the flow of air in and out of his lungs. It's in the quiet that he becomes aware of a different feeling, so strange that it takes him several minutes to decipher: the surreal sensation that he has two distinct heartbeats, pulsing together in perfect rhythm within his chest.

He lets his breath out slowly, shifting onto his uninjured side, and freezes when he realizes he isn't alone. In what is normally an empty corner between bedstead and window, there stands a chair, tall-backed and worn. Lancelot sits in that chair, with his chin drooping onto his chest and his eyes heavily closed. Asleep.

Despite the confusion and questions filling Arthur's head— despite the strange sensation of his own heartbeat doubled behind his ribs—Arthur smiles. It's not often that he can watch Lancelot unnoticed, and he indulges in the opportunity now. There's a hint of trouble on Lancelot's handsome face even in sleep, but such worry is only reasonable. The fact that he's here in Arthur's chambers, exhausted enough to fall asleep at his vigil, is proof of Lancelot's concern.

Arthur wonders how long he's been unconscious himself, though he's not quite ready to wake Lancelot and ask.

Lancelot's demeanor is every bit as somber in sleep as it is when the man is awake. His face is striking, deeply lined with cares, and from his left ear he bears a faint scar along a clean-shaven jaw. His hair is the most changed of all his features, gone from rich brown to gleaming silver in only a short span of years. More than once he's put the blame of it at Arthur's feet, always with a glimmer of mischief in his eye. It's the closest Lancelot ever comes to smiling.

Slumped forward as he is, Lancelot's hair falls pale across his brow. There's no sign of his customary armor. He hardly looks combat-ready in his dark leggings and dull tunic, but his sword sits propped against the stone wall beside him. Even in sleep Lancelot protects his king.

"Lancelot," Arthur says at last, pushing himself upright and leaning against the ornate headboard. Lancelot stirs, and that unfamiliar feeling in Arthur's chest falters, his plural heartbeats speeding as un-summoned relief rises alongside. Arthur blinks in confusion, but holds quiet. Lancelot's eyes are open now, and locked on him with an intensity that makes it difficult to breathe.

Silence stretches just long enough to be uncomfortable, and then Lancelot rises. He reaches for his sword as he moves, ties the scabbard to his belt, and inclines his head in something like a bow.

"I'll tell the Lady Merlin that you've woken." Lancelot's voice is rough-edged with sleep, but his movements are familiar precision.

Arthur doesn't want him to go, and he moves with a speed that surprises both of them, reaching out to grab Lancelot by the wrist. He stares up, startled at an even stronger surge of feeling in his chest, volatile and indecipherable. Lancelot shakes his arm free with a sharp gesture, and the look on his face stops the protest in Arthur's throat.

Despite every instinct screaming that he needs Lancelot to stay, Arthur lets him go.

By the time Merlin arrives, Arthur has already summoned a servant to draw a hot bath. The wooden tub has been carried in and placed near the fire, and several attendants come and go, carrying hot water up from the kitchens. Outside the narrow windows, the sun has grudgingly begun to set, and candlelight joins the hearth in casting the room alight. Two more servants are changing the bed linens, another carrying food to the table by the far wall. Arthur spares each of them a nod of gratitude but keeps to himself near the window. The cool air doesn't bother him. He still feels heavy with bone-deep fatigue, and the faintest ache throbs in his shoulder.

Arthur watches the sky and the darkening parapets below. It's beside the window that Merlin joins him. Her white hair is loose and clean, and it gusts carelessly in the low breeze. Merlin's eyes are paler than when Arthur was a child, and he knows her sight is failing. Her mind and magic remain sharply honed, though, and there are none in Camelot so foolish as to suggest blindness will weaken her.

"Your highness," she greets him, dipping low in an elegant curtsy. When she straightens there is warm fondness in her expression. Arthur recognizes exasperation in the subtle twitch at one corner of her mouth. She's clearly displeased to find him out of bed, but knows better than to chastise him.

"I should be dead." Arthur keeps his tone bland by willpower alone. These are not words easily spoken, but he says them without trembling. Merlin's expression sobers, and her mouth presses into a thin line.

"Yet here you stand," she says with an air of unrepentant challenge.

"Thanks to you?"

She nods. "And to Lancelot."

"How?" he asks quietly, for Merlin's ears alone. "Something tells me I haven't been asleep long enough to heal from so grave a wound. Tell me, Merlin. How many days since Camlann?"

"Only three, my lord," she says just as softly. "And the how of it is... complicated."

"Merlin," he admonishes. He's impatient for answers, and a note of severity creeps into his voice.

"It was a dangerous gamble, sire, and I make no apology for it. Until you woke, there was no knowing if the enchantment would hold." She turns away from him now, facing the window and the bruise-purple sky. "I invoked a magic older and more powerful than my own."

"A magic strong enough to heal a mortal wound?" Arthur asks, skeptical even to his own ears.

"No." Merlin shakes her head. "A magic to lend you the strength of another. To give you a fighting chance. Perhaps you have noticed something of that strength? A hint of someone else's will? A heartbeat that is not your own?"

"Yes." Arthur gapes at her. "And other things. Feelings."

Merlin nods, a reluctant smile tugging at her mouth. "Lancelot is strong in both body and soul. He would never let you die while it was within his power to save you. It is not my magic, but his strength, that has allowed you to heal."

"Does it hurt him?" Arthur tries to mask his alarm, but Merlin's expression softens to sympathy.

"It tires him. But no, it does not hurt him." She turns toward Arthur and briefly touches his wounded shoulder. Her hand is perfectly steady. Then she folds her arms before her. Something in her stance speaks of hesitation, and Arthur's eyes narrow.

"What are you not telling me? If it doesn't hurt him, why do you say it was dangerous?"

"Because there was no guarantee even Lancelot could save you," Merlin admits, watching Arthur closely. "He risked his own life, sire. Had you died...."

"I'd have taken him with me," Arthur realizes.

"There's no point being angry about it," Merlin interrupts the ember of rage coming alive in Arthur's chest. Her gentle tone instantly calms him. "You did not die. Lancelot is perfectly safe. And while he is bound to you, it is not only his strength you will share. The connection runs deep. You can sense the way his heartbeat guides your own? Yes, of course you can. And the feelings you spoke of are almost certainly his as well."

"Does he know all this?"

"Of course." Merlin arches one pale eyebrow. "It would hardly have been fair to leave him in the dark."

Arthur turns his focus inward, toward the strange mirror of heartbeats inside him. But for all that he's deliberately searching, he finds no hint of emotion beyond his own. "Why can't I feel him now?"

"He is not near enough at hand, I suspect. You need not worry, sire. He won't have gone far. He must stay close, or the enchantment will fail."

"Then it isn't permanent? This enchantment?"

"No." Merlin leans back against the high window ledge. Over her shoulder, the sky has lost the last of its color, leaving only dull darkness behind. "I will remove the charm when I am confident of your safety."

Arthur blinks in confusion, his brow furrowing. "I don't understand. I feel fine."

"Your wounds have healed," Merlin concedes. "But that is not the whole of the danger you face. Mordred's blade was poisoned. I dare not break the spell until this too has passed."

"And how long will that be?" Arthur presses.

"Soon enough, sire. You need only be patient."

When finally Lancelot returns, the hour is gone past midnight. Arthur is alone in his chambers, servants and wooden tub gone, hearth stoked high to combat the night's chill. Merlin admonished him to sleep when she left, but Arthur feels as though he's been sleeping for a century. He is tired, but he's also restless, and the thought of returning to his bed is untenable.

He knows even before the sound of the knock that Lancelot has come. He can feel it in his chest, where the twin heartbeats have grown louder, and he opens the door at the first rap on heavy wood. Lancelot stands in the silent corridor, dressed as he was before. His sword hangs at his side, and his hand rests loosely around the grip. Only sporadic torchlight illuminates the hall behind him, and the deep shadows make his face severe.

"You're still awake." The disapproval in Lancelot's tone is faint but discernible. Arthur doesn't call him out for the subtle insolence. He simply stands aside, allowing Lancelot through the door and closing it behind him. There's no reason of security for him to lock the door, but Arthur slides the bolt home anyway. Something tells him that whatever Lancelot has come for, it's a conversation better kept private.

"Clearly I'm not the only one who finds himself restless,"

Arthur retorts, crossing his arms and quirking an eyebrow in imitation of Merlin's favorite expression. He doesn't intend the words as a rebuke, but neither is it Lancelot's place to chastise him.

Lancelot's back is to Arthur, his posture tight. His feelings—those that Arthur can sense—are so guarded as to be opaque. There's no mistaking the fact that Lancelot is troubled, but beyond that it's impossible to surmise.

Arthur's tone gentles when he says, "I should thank you. Merlin told me what happened."

Instead of easing the tension in those broad shoulders, Arthur's words make Lancelot turn sharply on his heel. Lancelot's cheek twitches, his jaw clenches, and Arthur abruptly recognizes the dominant feeling in the mess of borrowed emotions.

Anger. Lancelot is furious. It takes Arthur conscious effort not to startle back from such unwonted rage.

"What were you thinking?" Lancelot demands, fire flashing in gray eyes.

The question borders on treason, and Arthur's perfect posture tightens. "Mind your position, Lancelot," he says, in the crisp tones that set lesser men groveling. Lancelot only looms toward him, towering over Arthur and seeming even taller than usual. Arthur holds his ground. He will not be cowed by anyone, even the very best of his knights.

"You were *careless*," Lancelot snaps. He's no longer touching his sword. His hands have curled into helpless fists at his sides, and his voice rises sharply when he continues, "Your escort cannot protect you if you deliberately evade them!"

Arthur *hadn't* deliberately evaded his escort at Camlann, but he doesn't bother arguing the point. Instead he gapes, confounded in the face of Lancelot's unaccustomed anger.

"You can't *scold* me," Arthur protests. "I'm the king!"

His pricked pride is distracting enough that it takes him a moment to see through it, to the true source of Lancelot's fury. When he does, his own ruffled feathers smooth, and the fight bleeds quickly out of him.

"You're not angry at me," Arthur realizes aloud. He peers up into Lancelot's face, takes in the heavy line of his brow, the creases at the corners of his narrowed eyes, the unhappy line of his mouth. Arthur meets the piercing intensity of gray eyes and says, "You're upset with yourself. Because..." His own brow furrows as he works it through. "Because you weren't at my side?"

Lancelot growls, an inarticulate sound that sends a tremble along Arthur's spine, and then he shoves Arthur hard against the heavy door. Arthur's back collides uncomfortably with sturdy wood, and the faded hurt in his shoulder twinges dully. There's something helpless and furious in Lancelot's eyes as he holds Arthur pinned. Arthur can decipher nothing through the wild tumult of Lancelot's emotions, though he feels them louder than ever with Lancelot's hands on him. He doesn't try to free himself. Instead he stands patiently, caution and stillness, and waits for Lancelot to speak.

"You could have died." A surge of feeling matches the pained truth in Lancelot's voice, and Arthur aches with the honesty of it.

"I didn't," he says, wishing he could ease that ache for both of them.

"You *should* have." Lancelot's eyes flash with a fresh spike of fear. "You were mortally wounded. If Merlin hadn't—"

"But she *did*," Arthur cuts him off with warm finality. His eyes cut away, downward, and he glimpses a golden chain at Lancelot's throat. The chain—a necklace, really—has slipped free from the collar of Lancelot's tunic, and at the end hangs a purple jewel that Arthur doesn't recognize. Lancelot has never favored gems, but the incongruity isn't what stops Arthur short.

The jewel is glowing. Not just glowing, he realizes, but pulsing faintly with a rapid rhythm.

A rhythm that matches exactly the suddenly racing heartbeats twining in Arthur's chest.

He reaches without thought. The gold-set gem is warm to the touch and heavy in his hand. Arthur stares at it for several seconds, mesmerized by the intimate pulse of light. Lancelot is perfectly motionless, still holding him inescapably against the chamber door, and Arthur does his best not to think about anything beyond the bauble in his hand.

It seems an eternity later when Lancelot speaks. "If we had lost you, sire...." He doesn't finish the sentence. Maybe he can't. Arthur's own voice is stuck somewhere deep and fractured, and it's with unexpected difficulty that he raises his eyes from the amulet to find Lancelot watching him. The air is suddenly too thick to breathe, and Arthur is drowning in a tangle of emotions that aren't his own.

Then, in a jarring instant of clarity, one clear feeling breaks through the tumult.

Arthur recognizes that feeling: warm, sharp, fiercely intimate, and far more complicated than the simple loyalty of friendship. It's almost an exact match for the things Arthur feels for Lancelot, when he's alone and weak and tired of being a king.

Arthur is too startled to guard his expression as these understandings find him, and Lancelot's eyes widen in answer. The amulet falls forgotten from Arthur's fingers, and he raises his hand to Lancelot's face.

Arthur's touch is hesitant, and hopeful, and a little bit terrified.

It's enough to snap Lancelot free of the panic freezing him in place. He jerks back as though Arthur has burned him, taking his hands guiltily off of his king. His retreat takes him to the farthest corner of the room, between the enormous desk and the narrow window behind it. He turns his back to Arthur, bracing his palms against the stone ledge. When Arthur follows, approaching cautiously, Lancelot doesn't acknowledge him except to tense where he stands.

Lancelot continues to stare fiercely out the window, even when Arthur stops beside him. He ignores the hand Arthur sets to his arm, and Arthur drops the hand again, feeling confused and defeated.

"Forgive me," Lancelot says when Arthur is no longer touching him. "I know it's not my place. And you must believe, I would never...."

But he tapers off without finishing, and after an uncertain moment Arthur asks, "Never what?"

The question makes Lancelot flinch, but he takes his hands off the window. A moment later and he actually looks at Arthur, wounded resignation in the cloudy gray of his eyes.

"You are my king," Lancelot answers helplessly, and the ache beneath the words almost sends Arthur to his knees.

He keeps his footing and reaches out instead, twisting his fingers in the front of Lancelot's tunic and tugging him down into a kiss that startles them both.

It ends almost instantly, though Arthur can't figure out how to loosen his grip. They stare at each other in matching surprise, their shared heartbeats speeding frantically. Arthur has never seen Lancelot's eyes so wide, or his face so open with shock. Now he thinks on it, he can't remember ever seeing Lancelot caught off guard. In a hundred other circumstances the result could be humorous, but not here. Not tonight. Not in the painful seconds that are stretching between them, making Arthur second guess actions he never gave a first thought to.

It's Lancelot who ultimately breaks the stalemate. He moves, not in retreat, but in a possessive surge forward. He reaches for Arthur, and the roughness of his hands—one cupping the back of Arthur's skull, the other closing around his hip—ignites a thrill of heat beneath Arthur's skin. Arthur's eyes close as he's crushed against the unyielding muscle of Lancelot's chest.

There is nothing fleeting in this kiss. Arthur offers no resistance to the desperation in Lancelot's touch. His hands grasp more tightly at Lancelot's tunic, and his lips part for the possessive thrust of Lancelot's tongue. He feels himself pushed abruptly backward, and the edge of his desk bumps hard against the backs of Arthur's thighs, stopping and trapping him. The pommel of Lancelot's sword bangs against the wood, a jarring noise that neither of them heeds. Arthur breathes a needy sound and tilts his head for a deeper kiss.

When it ends they're both breathing hard. Lancelot's fingers gentle where they still curl at the nape of Arthur's neck, but he doesn't let go. He doesn't back away.

When Arthur at last opens his eyes, he finds Lancelot already watching him.

Questions spark in that piercing stare, and there's uncertainty in the set to his jaw. Lancelot's lips are parted, and his gaze keeps dropping to Arthur's mouth before jerking quickly upward again. The hand at Arthur's hip slides back, almost tentatively, to press palm-flat over his spine, and Arthur draws a slower breath.

Disbelief mingles with a greedier sensation, and Arthur recognizes the feelings for his own. He can sense the truth of them reflected in Lancelot, in that confusing place where they're tangled up in each other, but alongside them he recognizes something more cautious. Nothing at all like regret, but a sense of duty that might send Lancelot running just as surely.

"I want you to stay," Arthur says, embarrassed at the breathless need in his own voice. Lancelot's gaze sharpens, and his fingers at Arthur's nape tighten warningly.

"We both know that would be unwise."

"Yes," Arthur agrees. He untwists his fingers from rough fabric and frames Lancelot's face with his hands. "Stay anyway." He's never wanted anything as urgently as he wants Lancelot in his bed tonight.

When Lancelot kisses him a third time, it is a slower, gentler kiss. Cautious exploration now, where before every touch was demanding fire. Arthur presses full against him, pleading for more without the benefit of words. With only leggings and tunics between them, there's no mistaking Lancelot's arousal. Arthur's own cock is rising just as surely, heavy and hard between his legs. If Lancelot leaves now, Arthur fears he will go mad.

He gasps when Lancelot releases his mouth in favor of tracing a line of kisses down the side of Arthur's throat. There's the grazing hint of teeth, a cautious tease only. Lancelot may want to mark him—Arthur may be able to feel the desire vividly between them—but they both know better. Even so, Lancelot's mouth is maddening heat on Arthur's skin.

Arthur slips a hand into the nonexistent space between their bodies, quests downward and cups the hard heat of Lancelot's cock through taut fabric.

Lancelot breathes rough curses against Arthur's throat at the touch. His hips jerk forward, pressing his arousal into Arthur's cupped hand and crushing him against the edge of the desk. Arthur grins and uses the same hand, awkward at this trapped angle, to fumble at the laces of Lancelot's leggings, loosening them impatiently.

The desk, huge and sturdy behind him, doesn't budge when Lancelot abruptly shoves Arthur down onto his back. Strong hands hold him down, and Lancelot looms above him. Fierce fire glints in Lancelot's eyes.

"Bed, perhaps?" There is both heat and humor in Lancelot's tone. "Unless you would prefer I take you right here."

Arthur's mind flashes brightly on that image, and he's tempted. But he is also desperate to make this last, and ultimately he summons breath enough to answer, "Bed. Yes."

He still feels lost when Lancelot takes a step back, releasing him and letting him up. Arthur rounds the desk and backs toward the bed with impatient speed, dragging his own loose tunic over his head as he moves. When he drops it carelessly to the floor, he sees that Lancelot has done the same. Arthur trips, distracted by the view, and it's only by luck that he lands on the high edge of the bed instead of the cold stone floor.

There's silver hair scattered across Lancelot's bare chest, along with a patchwork of old scars and newer bruises fading from the violence at Camlann. Firelight catches on muscle that puts Arthur's own lean body to shame, and though this is not the first time Arthur has seen Lancelot in such a state of undress, it *is* the first time he truly allows himself to look.

Lancelot's laces are already undone, and as he reaches the edge of the bed he unties the belt from his hips and sets his sword upright against the wall. He takes up Arthur's entire field of vision now, standing so close, and it's with difficulty that Arthur raises his eyes to Lancelot's face.

He finds Lancelot staring down at him with a hunger Arthur

can feel mirrored in his chest. The feeling amplifies between them, a jolt of raw want, and Arthur can't tell if it's magic or simply a need too long ignored. He doesn't care. He pushes his feet off of the floor to slide properly onto the bed, scooting toward the headboard. He watches rapt as Lancelot maneuvers out of his leggings and leaves them behind, then follows Arthur onto the bed, knees dimpling the bedclothes beneath his weight.

The sight of Lancelot naked is an even headier distraction than the sight of him shirtless, and Arthur catches his own lower lip between his teeth to keep quiet. He only has a moment, seconds at most, to appreciate the view before Lancelot is upon him. Impatient hands push him down into the pillows, and then Lancelot reaches for Arthur's laces in turn, tearing them in his hurry. Arthur doesn't complain; he is equally anxious to be naked, and he twists helpfully beneath Lancelot's efforts, lifting his legs to make it easier for Lancelot to tear the garment away.

Lancelot breathes a satisfied sound as he throws the last vestige of their clothing to the floor. Then, instead of joining him as Arthur expects, Lancelot braces one elbow on the bed, one arm across Arthur's hips, and takes the straining length of Arthur's cock into his mouth.

Arthur gasps, a greedy sound that shatters the quiet air. His entire body tries instinctively to arch upward into that wet, perfect heat. Lancelot's strength keeps him steady, holds him down easily as Lancelot takes him deeper. Teasing at first, then offering harder suction as Arthur's length nudges at the back of his throat. Arthur makes a more plaintive sound, and his fingers thread thoughtlessly in the soft silver of Lancelot's hair.

Lancelot draws back, tongue pressing along the underside of the shaft, then takes Arthur deep once more.

He works with a skill that might inspire jealousy if Arthur weren't so busy coming to pieces. Fortunately Arthur doesn't have enough extra space in his brain to think about Lancelot doing this with someone else. His entire world has narrowed to Lancelot's mouth on him, Lancelot's hands holding him down.

He won't last, and he tries to find the coherence to say so, but all that comes out of his mouth is a wild groan of release when sensation carries him over the edge.

Lancelot is nearly smiling when Arthur manages to open his eyes. A hint of smugness tints his fond expression as he slips upward along the bed and covers Arthur with his body. Arthur welcomes the kiss that follows, the taste of himself on Lancelot's tongue, almost as much as he welcomes Lancelot's warm weight atop him. Arthur's hands slide down strong shoulders, along the smooth-muscled planes of spine and flank. Lancelot's own hands are restless, every touch edging toward frantic as he catches Arthur's lower lip between his teeth and then eases the faint sting with his tongue.

Arthur is half out of his mind when Lancelot props himself on one elbow to meet Arthur's eyes.

Lancelot's cheeks are flushed, his expression stormy with need, and he starts to ask, "Do you have anything to—?"

"Here," Arthur interrupts, already reaching for a niche in the intricate headboard. He finds the vial easily by touch, though it's been months at least since he last had need of it. He presses the vial, still stoppered, into Lancelot's hand.

The look Lancelot gives him then is eloquent, but Arthur doesn't need it to make sense of the wordless question. He can sense jealous curiosity through their shared connection.

Arthur arches a single eyebrow and asks, "Where is it written that a king must spend his nights alone?"

He barely has time to wonder if this might pose a problem before Lancelot kisses him once more, lingering and slow. Spent or not, Arthur's cock twitches with renewed interest.

He doesn't protest when Lancelot lets go of him and backs down the bed, nudging Arthur's knee aside so that he can settle between Arthur's legs. Lancelot kneels there, unstopping the vial, glancing at Arthur for only an instant before pouring slick oil over his fingers.

He touches Arthur with maddening care. Lancelot's fingers are steady and confident when they press inside him, an intimate ache as he slips them deeper, loosening Arthur's body for what comes next. His free hand closes around Arthur's cock, the warm length stiff as though Arthur hasn't already spent himself once tonight. Lancelot strokes him softly at first, in time with thrusting fingers. His touch firms by degrees, carrying Arthur deliberately to the edge and keeping him there. All the while Arthur can feel Lancelot's eyes on him, burning through him as Arthur comes apart. There's something possessive in the way Lancelot is watching him and in the bright burst of feeling that the enchantment sends directly to Arthur.

Like he already knows just how thoroughly Arthur belongs to him.

Arthur is on the verge of begging when Lancelot's fingers slide free, and he gasps a fractured noise. He doesn't fear anyone overhearing through the thick stone walls, but it's an embarrassing sound, needy and desperate. As Lancelot's weight covers him once more, Arthur wonders if it's only his own need he's feeling so acutely. The hot length of Lancelot's arousal nudges between his thighs, and there is unmasked hunger in Lancelot's eyes when their gazes lock. Their twin heartbeats are rising chaos somewhere deep and secret, and Arthur draws a shaky breath, touches Lancelot's face with reverent fingers.

"Please," Arthur whispers. It's only the third time in his life he's spoken the word.

There's an uncoordinated moment, as Lancelot pours more oil into his palm and reaches down to slick his cock. Arthur intercepts the vial, not quite empty, and fumbles the stopper back into place. He doesn't try and return it to its discreet hideaway once sealed, but tosses it aside, out of the way toward the far edge of the bed. He doesn't much care where it lands. He has better priorities.

Lancelot's breath is warm along Arthur's jaw. His lips brush Arthur's ear, and his voice is barely above a whisper. "Are you ready?"

Arthur groans in answer, tangling his fingers in Lancelot's hair and dragging him in for a frantic kiss. Lancelot takes his own length in hand then, positioning himself between Arthur's thighs. The teasing nudge becomes deliberate pressure as the blunt head presses inside, and Arthur breaks the kiss to gasp against Lancelot's throat. He nudges forward with his hips, taking Lancelot deeper, urging more, and Lancelot groans a curse into Arthur's skin as he jerks forward, driving in to the hilt in a single thrust. There's pain—of course there's pain—but it's fleeting, quickly overwhelmed by more familiar pleasure and by a bright surge of borrowed emotion in Arthur's chest. Satisfaction, desire, overwhelming elation. Arthur gasps again, this time from the force of Lancelot's feelings rushing through him.

They move, awkwardly at first, learning each other, learning how they fit together. The amulet, still hanging by its chain around Lancelot's neck, bumps warmly against Arthur's chest. Lancelot's hands are eager strength everywhere they touch, restless, as though desperate to leave nowhere unexplored. Arthur's own hands tremble, and he clutches at Lancelot's back, relishing the bunch and flex of powerful muscle beneath his palms. He arches to meet every thrust, rolling his hips to take Lancelot deeper still.

They find their balance, the perfect give-and-take, and together rush over the edge of release.

There's an unsteadiness to the quiet that settles around them after. The fire burns low, spreading heavier shadows throughout Arthur's chambers. The air has gone chill with the fading hearth, and both Arthur and Lancelot have settled beneath the heavy bedclothes. Lancelot lies on his back, the purple jewel pulsing sedately where it rests above his heart.

Arthur's own restlessness cools and calms as he curls against Lancelot's side. He rests his head on Lancelot's shoulder and drapes an arm across his stomach, breathing in time with the rise and fall of Lancelot's chest. He becomes aware again of the ache in his shoulder, but the weak discomfort barely warrants notice.

The silence is both intimate and cautious, and it's Lancelot who reluctantly breaks it.

"You know I can't really stay."

"I know," Arthur agrees, though he wishes he didn't have to. There will be consequences if Lancelot is discovered in his bed. Arthur is the king, but even a king is not above scrutiny. "We have time yet." Scant hours, yes, but time nonetheless.

The first of Arthur's servants will arrive just before sunup, and there are four hours at least until then. For all the sated satisfaction humming beneath Arthur's skin, he's in no danger of falling asleep—and from the sense of Lancelot entwined with their steadying heartbeats, Arthur knows he is not alone.

It's proof of Arthur's trust, and of his faith in Lancelot, that Arthur finally asks, "What happens now?"

Lancelot is silent for a very long time. He trails warm fingers up the length of Arthur's spine, cards them through the dark mess of Arthur's hair. Arthur wishes he could decipher clearer thoughts through the connection between them. He doesn't know what to make of this silence, or of the complicated tangle of Lancelot's feelings running fitfully beneath.

When Arthur shifts, intending to move away and offer what space and peace he can, Lancelot's arms tighten about him and prevent any such retreat. A possessive ember burns brighter as he tugs Arthur more firmly against him, and Lancelot exhales slowly.

"I think, sire," he says at last, sounding exhausted but giving off a faint pulse of hope somewhere more intimate, "that what happens now depends on you."

"No." Arthur lays one palm flat over Lancelot's heart, pushing himself up to look Lancelot in the eye. "This is not the king's purview. It is far more complicated than that."

"I suppose it is," Lancelot concedes. He reaches up to tuck a dark strand of hair behind Arthur's ear. His expression is heavily somber.

Arthur wants to kiss him, abruptly and with a jarring desperation. It takes conscious will to hold motionless instead. "I'm asking what *you* want."

"You already know what I want," Lancelot protests, and his brow creases faintly.

"I know what you feel. It is not necessarily the same." He peers down at Lancelot, trying to read straight into his soul. "I don't wish to put you in an untenable position," Arthur says softly. "I know very well how you feel tonight, but what of tomorrow? And the day after that? What of all the days that follow, when I am king first, and all else must come second?" *Even you*, he cannot bear to say aloud, though they both understand the truth of it.

Instead of answering at once, Lancelot twines his fingers in Arthur's hair and tugs him down for a kiss that is harsh with need. Arthur parts his lips for Lancelot's tongue, clings to him with a desperation all his own. He doesn't resist when Lancelot pushes upward beneath him, nudging Arthur onto his back, reversing their positions and pressing him down into the pillows. The bedclothes slip and twist with the movement, pooling at Lancelot's waist and allowing cool air to ghost across warm skin.

It's with obvious reluctance that Lancelot breaks the kiss, propping one elbow on the pillow beside Arthur's head so that they can meet each other's eyes.

"I know you belong, body and soul, to Camelot." Lancelot's voice is heavy with the weight of reverence. "And I vow to you that I will never ask for more than you can give."

"You *deserve* more." Arthur's throat tightens around the words, but he forces himself to speak them.

"As do you," Lancelot answers quietly.

Then they are kissing, holding on too tightly. Even when they stop, Arthur finds he can't recall how to breathe, and it's long moments before he manages to open his eyes. Of course he finds Lancelot watching him, and Arthur doesn't know what to say.

"I am not a selfless man, sire," Lancelot admits, and for all that his tone is still heavy with meaning, there's a hint of smile in his eyes now. "Nor am I of a sharing disposition. I will allow Camelot's superior claim, but I would not take kindly to anyone else in your bed."

Bright feeling cracks open in Arthur's chest, and he finds himself smiling without thought. His blood warms pleasantly despite the chill of the room, perhaps because of Lancelot's words, or perhaps thanks to the warm weight of Lancelot's body, the intimate heat of bare skin.

"Why would I invite someone else to my bed?" Arthur asks, letting the warmth tinge his voice and turn his question into an invitation. "Now that I've had you, who else could possibly satisfy me?"

Lancelot only growls, and kisses him again.

Destiny
Katya Harris

A few days before the Battle of Camlann

She was everything he was not. Mordred knew that just by looking
at her. The golden light to his brooding darkness. With her
buttercup-yellow hair tumbling to her waist in a tangle of curls
and her creamy, sun-kissed skin, she glowed in the summer sun.
Walking along the path with willowy grace, the skirt of her simple
tunic dress swinging around her ankles, she was innocence and
sensuality, and Mordred couldn't take his eyes from her.

"Sire, we don't have time for this."

If Mordred had had a dagger in his hand he would have
stabbed Drust with it. "We have time for whatever I say we have
time for," he growled.

Drust wasn't deterred. Fool. "But sire, the king could return
any day. Your mother—"

"Can go to the Devil as you will if you don't cease your prattle."
Mordred glared at him and knew there was murder in his eyes
when the large knight paled. "You will do as I have told you to do.
I am your master, not my mother." He spat the last word, all the
hatred in his soul laid bare in that moment. "Now, unless you want
me to feed your corpse to the carrion crows, obey my orders."

Drust didn't protest again, although his jaw firmed with
resentment at his treatment. Kicking his horse forward, he left the
cover of the trees where they were concealed and rode toward the
slender figure in the distance. Mordred waited a few moments and
then followed at a more sedate pace. His eyes kept careful track of
Drust's movements as he came up behind the woman, and even
though Mordred knew what was going to happen, even though
he had ordered the other knight to do it, he still caught his breath
in alarm when Drust's horse clipped her shoulder and sent her

tumbling to the ground. Riding on like nothing had happened, Drust carried on up the path. With a grim smile, Mordred spurred his mount to go faster, pulling it to a halt and leaping off as he came alongside the fallen woman. Going to his knees beside her, he gathered her into his arms.

"My lady, are you well?"

Eyes the pale green of spring's first shoots blinked up at him dazedly. When she'd fallen, she must have struck her head on a rock; there was a bruise at her hairline, dark color already beginning to stain her pale skin. Mordred promised to give Drust a similar wound when he saw him next.

"Wh-what happened?"

Mordred's anger eased, soothed away by her husky voice. He smiled at her. "A rider knocked you down. Do you remember?"

The smooth skin of her forehead wrinkled a little as she frowned. She winced as the movement pulled on her bruise. "Y-yes, I think s-so. Didn't he st-stop?"

"No, the knave didn't," Mordred answered truthfully. "It was fortunate I was nearby. I hate to think of you being alone when you needed help."

A tremble shivered through her body. "Thank you, my lord. You're very kind."

He really wasn't, but Mordred wasn't about to tell her that. "I'm just glad I could be of assistance, my lady. Here, let me help you up." He didn't bother to get her to her own feet, instead using his great strength to lift her into his arms as he stood up. She gasped, her small hands clinging to his shoulders.

"My lord!"

"Hush. Let me take care of you."

"But—"

Mordred didn't allow her to protest any more. Lifting her onto the back of his horse, he settled her in front of the pommel before swinging up into the saddle behind her. His arms went around her, holding her in place as he reached for the reins.

"Where is your home?" As if he didn't already know.

Her hand shook as she pointed in the direction she had been walking. "There."

The small dwelling was not that far at all, but Mordred rode forward at a plodding pace. "If you feel unwell, tell me. Head wounds can be treacherous."

The woman's hands were wrapped in the horse's mane, her knuckles bone-white beneath her sun-kissed skin. Mordred could feel how she trembled against him, smell her fear mingling with the sweetly floral scent that clung to her. "Truly, you do not need to accompany me home, my lord. I will be quite well." Her hand went to the bruise on her head and she couldn't stop a wince.

"Yes," Mordred said, dryly. "You look the epitome of health." She opened her mouth, no doubt to object again, and instead of kissing her as he wanted, he continued, "Nothing you can say will deter me, my lady. I will see you safely home."

Her mouth shut with a click of teeth. They were nearly halfway there, Mordred enjoying the feel of her in his arms even if his hard cock was uncomfortable beneath his hose, when she said, "I've seen you before, haven't I, my lord? In the village?"

"Yes, I think so." He knew so. Passing through her village a few days ago, she had been the only thing that Mordred had really seen. His first sight of her, as she laughingly haggled with another villager for some cloth, had been like a blow to his own head. The shock of it had resonated through him like the clanging of a bell, and, blinking, he had felt like he had finally woken up. She had been in his thoughts ever since, and now she was in his arms.

"What are you doing here?" She blushed, her pale cheeks glowing with sudden rosy color as she realized how blunt her question sounded. "I mean, what brings you to our village, my lord? Are you a servant of the king?"

"I am a knight," Mordred said. He could not bring himself to lie and say he served Arthur. That was a falsehood even his talent for deception could not stretch to.

"Well, you certainly came to my rescue, my lord," she said, a bit of brightness returning to her pale face. "Thank you, Sir—?"

"Mordred. I am Sir Mordred, and I am at your service, my lady."

She giggled at his gallantry, a happy sound that caused a strange sensation in Mordred's chest. "Well met then, Sir Mordred. Thank you for your help."

"You're welcome." His deep voice dropped even lower, a huskiness roughening the edges of his words. Desire was a vine winding through his body, piercing every organ, constricting every muscle. He wanted her clear down to his bones, and the next time she said his name he wanted her to be screaming it as she climaxed around his thrusting cock.

"What's your name?" Of all the things he had learned about her as he'd followed her for the past few days, her name wasn't one of them.

"Carys."

"Beautiful," he whispered.

Carys's eyes darted up to look into his. The blush on her cheeks deepened, and her dark pink tongue peeked out from between her parted lips to lick at the bottom one.

Mordred couldn't help the sound he made then, a low rumble that bordered on a growl. He sounded like a feral beast, a wolf, and Carys's eyes widened and her skin paled as she stared at him.

"We're here."

She blinked, the long lengths of her eyelashes sweeping against the upper curve of her cheeks. "What?"

Mordred reined his horse to a stop. "Your home?"

She startled, her gaze jumping to the small dwelling by the path. This time it was embarrassment that colored her cheeks. "Yes, of course."

Dismounting, Mordred put his hands around her slim waist and lifted her down. He made sure to keep her close as he lowered her to the ground, the front of her body rubbing against his. When her feet finally touched the ground she was pressed up close against him. She was breathing hard, her breasts pushing against the muscled planes of his chest. Her nipples were hard; Mordred could feel them as surely as she could feel the ridge of his erection digging into her stomach.

"My lord?" Carys's eyes were large green pools in her face. Her voice trembled.

"Do not be afraid." He tried to speak softly, to be reassuring, but he could not keep the harshness of command from his words. "I won't hurt you."

"Yes, my lord," she said, her voice barely louder than a whisper. She didn't believe him.

Mordred forced his reluctant hands to let her go. Stepping back, he gestured for her to go inside. She moved, but she kept her eyes on him as much as possible, turning away only at the last possible moment. It wasn't hard to see that he had frightened her. A feeling squirmed in Mordred's gut. He thought it might have been regret.

Tying his horse's reins to a nearby tree branch, Mordred followed her.

Opening the front door, Carys turned to him. Her spine was drawn up straight, the slender width of her shoulders tense. "Thank you, my lord, for bringing me home."

"My pleasure, my lady." Unable to help himself, Mordred moved closer. "All I ask is a drink. The day is hot."

Carys's mouth twitched downward, betraying her displeasure, but she opened the door, stepping aside to let him pass.

The inside of the house was dim and blessedly cool. It was just as small as it seemed on the outside, the door opening into one large room that held the hearth and a table surrounded by a motley assortment of chairs. Bunches of dried herbs hung from the ceiling rafters to dry, perfuming the still air with a pleasant floral aroma. On the table a bowl full of pears and apples sat, and a loaf of freshly baked bread. A curtained doorway in one corner of the room no doubt led to Carys's bedchamber.

Sitting on one of the chairs, Mordred watched Carys as she fetched a small pitcher of beer from a cabinet. Her hand shook as she poured the amber liquid into a cup. When she placed the cup in front of him, he caught her hand. There were calluses on her palm and rough patches on her fingers from hard work, but it was still soft as silk compared to his.

"I told you I wouldn't hurt you."

When she spoke, her voice was breathless. "Then what are you planning, my lord?"

"Seducing you."

Mordred could feel the shiver that went through her then, and his grip on her hand tightened before she could think to pull away. Slowly, he pulled her toward him, spreading his knees so she could stand between them.

"What if I don't want to be seduced?" There was sharpness to her words, a hint of anger that made him smile.

Bringing her hand to his mouth, Mordred brushed his lips over the center of her palm. "Then I'll have to convince you."

In a slow, wet glide Mordred licked the hollow of her cupped hand, tasting the sweet-saltiness of her skin. Carys's breath hitched and then released in a soft moan as he sank his teeth into the meat at the base of her thumb in a tender bite.

"I could be married."

Mordred stilled. Rolling his eyes up to look at her, he noted her flushed cheeks, the shine on her lips where she had just licked them. "But you're not, are you?"

Golden curls tumbled around her shoulders as she slowly shook her head. "No. Not anymore. He died." A trace of sadness clung to those last two words, and anger flared in Mordred's heart even as he felt a terrible gladness. He had known she was a widow—a few careful questions in the village had given him that knowledge—he just didn't like that another man had known her, touched her. But even if her husband had still been alive, Mordred wouldn't have cared. He would have come for her no matter how many husbands stood in his path. Never one to lie to himself, Mordred knew he would have quietly murdered the man if he hadn't already been conveniently dead.

"Then there is nothing to stand in our way," he said with quiet determination.

"I am not a harlot," she protested.

"I never thought you were," Mordred told her. She wouldn't

have been nearly as appealing if she were. It wasn't just her beauty that had caught Mordred's eye, it was her purity. She was clean, her hands and heart unstained by the darkness that had long ago swallowed his soul.

Turning his head, Mordred placed another lingering kiss in her palm. With gentle strength, he pulled her down to sit in his lap. She resisted a moment and then sat, perching on his thigh, her body stiff.

"Kiss me, Carys." Her name was a caress on his lips.

She stared at him, eyes wide and transfixed on his. She looked at him like a mouse looked at the snake, but she leaned closer. "What if I want you to stop?"

"Then I'll stop." For the first time in his life, Mordred prayed that he was telling the truth.

Staying still was the hardest thing he'd ever had to do. Carys's mouth was as sweet as perfectly ripe fruit as she pressed it lightly against his in a chaste kiss. Tension sang up Mordred's spine, his cock jerking hard between his legs. Instincts long ago honed to a sword's deadly sharpness screamed at him to take her. *No*, he whispered to himself as she continued to sip from his lips. He was not an animal and nor was he the demon some men called him before he sent them screaming to Hell, and for once in his misbegotten life he would act like it. For her.

The wet touch of her tongue gliding across the seam of his mouth almost undid that resolution. Mordred groaned, his arms tightening around her waist. Before he could stop himself, he slanted his mouth over hers and seized control of her kiss. His tongue surged into her mouth, hungry for the taste of her, and she submitted to him with a whimper, her hands coming up to grasp the heavy muscles of his shoulders, her fingernails pricking deep. He wanted to drown in her sweetness, die in the sea of desire that enveloped him. He kissed her, just that, and when she hesitantly kissed him back, her tongue dancing along his own, he wanted to tip back his head and roar in relieved triumph.

Clutching her to him, Mordred deepened their kiss. Tangling

one hand in her curls, he cupped her breast with the other. Carys gasped, breaking away to stare at him. Her lips were wet and swollen, stained red from his attentions.

Breathing hard, Mordred stared back at her. His thumb flicked over the taut bud of her nipple, and he watched, rapt, as she shivered beneath the caress. Her cheeks were rosy with arousal, the green of her eyes brilliant around the inky pools of her pupils. She squirmed slightly on his leg, the scent of her arousal starting to perfume the air.

Carys wanted him.

Bending his head, Mordred kissed the tip of her breast through the worn cloth of her dress. He licked at it, nibbled at it, and she wriggled against him even harder. Her hands moved from his shoulders to grasp the thick strands of his hair, holding him to her—as if he had any intention of stopping. He worshipped her covered breasts until he couldn't bear it anymore. The tie lacing the top of her dress closed succumbed to one firm tug of his hand. A brush of his fingers and the sleeves slipped down, exposing her shoulders and the tops of her breasts. Carys bit her bottom lip as he gently pulled the top of her dress down even further, but she didn't protest.

"Beautiful." Mordred breathed the word out on a hoarse sigh.

Her breasts were even more perfect than he'd thought they would be: plump and firm, capped with small, tightly furled nipples like dusky-pink rosebuds. The flush staining Carys's cheeks travelled downward to color the creamy skin of her chest. Beneath his gaze, her nipples turned redder, little berries inviting him to taste. Mordred didn't refuse.

They both moaned as he sucked her nipple into his mouth, and Carys didn't stop as he tormented the trembling mounds of her breasts. "My lord, please," she whimpered.

Cock throbbing with need, Mordred surged to his feet. Carys yelped, startled, and then made a soft noise of surrender as he laid her back on the table, her legs hanging over the edge. Standing between her spread thighs, Mordred ran his hands over her body in covetous strokes. She writhed under his touch, pushing her breasts into his palms whenever his hands touched them.

"Do you want me, Carys?"

She bit her lips hard before answering, the blush on her cheeks intensifying to a blazing red. "I do. I want you."

"Then you shall have me."

Stroking down over her hips and then her thighs, Mordred gathered up the skirt of her dress. Carys's breath stuttered when he lifted it up to her hips, revealing the treasure nestled between her thighs. Soft golden curls shielded her pretty cunny from Mordred's eyes, but they couldn't protect her from his mouth as he dropped to his knees and buried his face between her legs.

Carys cried out, shock seizing her body tight. She tried to close her legs, but Mordred's broad shoulders wedged them open. Her hands snatched at his hair, but he had felt worse pain in his life and for much worse reasons. Her resistance didn't last long anyway. The first lick of Mordred's tongue against the pearl of her sex and she melted with a shuddering moan.

Mordred's fingers dug into the soft flesh of Carys's thighs. She tasted so good, salty with a tang of honeyed sweetness. He lapped at the trembling flesh of her cunt, licking up the juices that spilled from her. When he sucked at the pulsing knot at the top of her slit, the tip of his tongue flicking over it, she cried out, her whole body convulsing as she reached her ultimate pleasure. There was a clatter and then several hollow thuds as the bowl of fruit was knocked to the floor by her flailing arms.

Surging to his feet, Mordred lifted up Carys's limp body and crushed his mouth to hers. She whimpered under the assault of his lips and tongue, but she feverishly returned the kisses that were flavored by the juices still clinging to his face.

Mordred's cock throbbed with urgency. His hands were rough as he tore the dress from her body. Stepping away from her to do the same with his own clothes was almost unbearable—except for the hungry look on Carys's face as she watched him disrobe. One side of Mordred's mouth tipped upward in a dark smile as he stood before her in resplendent nakedness. He had a warrior's body, heavy with muscle and scarred from combat. "Do you like what you see, my lady?" he challenged her. It was shocking to him, this need for her approval when before he had never cared what anyone had thought of him.

Carys's eyes burned a heated emerald green as she looked him over. Her breaths started to come harder, her plump breasts heaving with the force of them. "Yes," she murmured, huskily. "I do."

Mordred held his arms out to her. "Then come and embrace me."

Without hesitation she glided forward, rounded hips swaying. The last vestige of Mordred's control snapped.

Pulling Carys toward him, he lifted her up. Her legs went around his hips, trapping the rigid length of his erection against the slick flesh of her cunny. Mordred growled. Turning, he held her against the wall. Flexing his hips, he rubbed his cock through the wet folds of her sex. Carys shuddered hard, legs and arms clutching him to her.

Fire blazed on the edges of Mordred's mind, ran in liquid streams through his veins.

"I won't hurt you," he gasped out, and then with a flex of his hips he started pushing his cock inside her.

Heated wetness surrounded him, a glorious tightness that sent pleasure rilling up his spine. Gasping cries spilled from Carys's mouth as he thrust his way into her cunt and, greedy for every part of her, he sealed his mouth over hers to swallow them.

Carys's silken body rubbed against his as she writhed, trapped between his body and the wall. He wanted to hold her there forever as he fucked her, balanced on the knife's edge of pleasure. He never wanted it to end.

His body moved, ecstasy rushing over him in stronger and stronger waves, an unstoppable tide that would soon flood over him and carry him away. And mixed in with that pleasure was a hideous pain, a crack in his heart that Carys tore wide open without even knowing it.

He wanted her. Oh god, how he wanted her. Not for now or

the night, but forever. He wanted to hold her in his arms every day and every night. He wanted to know her, care for her. He wanted to love her and be loved by her in return. He wanted a family, happiness. The freedom of a life where he could choose his own destiny, where his future hadn't been sacrificed on the altar of his mother's ambitions and his father's weakness. A life where his mother hadn't seduced her brother to beget him, damning his soul before he had even been born.

Rage at the destiny smothering him sharpened the force of Mordred's thrusts. Carys broke away from his ravening kiss with a hoarse scream, her fingernails clawing deep into the muscles of his shoulders. "Mordred!" Her already tight cunny clenched around him like a fist, milking him as she climaxed.

Mordred's body couldn't resist following. Pleasure swept over him, a tide of fiery sensation that threatened to burn him alive. He roared in his release, his seed spurting from his cock in knee-weakening waves as he buried himself in Carys as deep as he could go.

It was over too soon. Through the thin walls of their chests, their hearts thudded against each other. Sweat stuck their skin together. *If only it could last,* Mordred thought.

Gathering up his tattered strength, Mordred carried Carys's boneless body through the curtained doorway to her bedchamber. Laying her on the bed, he lay beside her and held her close.

"Why me?" Her question was quiet.

"Because you're everything I'm not," Mordred answered truthfully. "Because you're everything I want."

Leaning up on her forearm, Carys looked down at him. She fairly glowed from their lovemaking. "I don't understand."

The only answer Mordred gave her was to curl his hand around her nape and draw her down for a kiss.

They made love twice more during the night, stopping only to replenish their strength with some of Carys's freshly baked bread and the fruit that was none the worse for wear from being knocked to the floor. They talked and they even laughed, and

Mordred swallowed the despair that yawned open within him for a life he would never have.

Just as dawn started to pink the sky, he woke her again by sliding his cock into the warm heaven of her body, loving her slowly and tenderly as the sun rose. When they were finished, Carys slid back into a deep sleep, a satisfied smile curling her lips, and Mordred left her bed forever. She never heard him when he whispered "I love you," into her ear before he strode out of the cottage, leaving what little remained of his heart nestled in the palm of her hand.

They were waiting for him in the clearing where he and Drust had watched Carys the day before. His knights' eyes were questioning until his glare murdered whatever curiosity they had.

Drust sidled his horse up next to Mordred's. "Sire, your mother is waiting and Arthur has been sighted on his way to Camelot. It's time."

Old, familiar rage scorched Mordred's soul. He wanted to burn the world in return. "Fine," he seethed. "Let's go kill my father, the king."

Under the Sign of the Dragon
Jean Roberta

My lord, the Duke of Cornwall, has accepted Christ Jesus as his savior for a score of years. As his lady, I have a duty to pray as he does before our people, whatever I believe in my heart. My lord's honor deserves no less.

How different things were when the Maiden, the Mother, and the Crone commanded us to follow our hearts. No man took offense if his lady held a paramour in her arms before the Beltane fires, nor would a good woman try to keep her wedded lord on a short tether throughout life. I remember a time when love was not confined, but I was a young maid who barely understood it. I was simply Igraine then, and I was too merry to be wise.

Now I wait alone behind the thick stone walls of Castle Tintagel for news of my lord Cornwall, and of the King I love beyond measure. They plan each other's destruction, and I fear for them both.

My reader, you who finds this after all has been resolved, please receive my tale with an open heart. In the hope of your merciful understanding, I shall lead you down the path that brought me here.

I hardly expected to wed at all, and certainly not before the age of twenty, but so it was to be. The Duke of Cornwall was a mighty lord who wished to gain the good will of all the nobility in neighboring realms, and such were my parents.

At our first meeting, he gazed at me with the kindness and the sorrow of a man who has seen forty winters and outlived the wife of his youth. "You may call me Geoffrey," he said, taking my hand, "if I may call you Igraine." Later, when we were alone, he swore on the Holy Book of his faith that he would never harm me while he lived.

I saw myself in his eyes as a young woman with thin shoulders and budlike breasts. My black hair and milky skin contrasted with his light-brown hair, flecked with grey, and the ruddy face of a man who has spent much time outdoors. I was not accustomed to wearing my hair bound up, nor my restless body encased in a silken gown. I did not wish to appear to my noble suitor as a child, but my young spirit seemed to delight him.

I wore a white gown for my wedding, embroidered with golden anchors and trimmed with French lace. I wore on my head a circlet of roses and ivy leaves, and I was attended by three maids all dressed in blue. Geoffrey was richly attired in purple, and his tunic bore a design of black Cornish choughs, their eyes and beaks cleverly worked in red. His own eyes looked as bright and observant as those of a wild bird. From his neck hung a gold pendant in the form of a cross, and this seemed to promise that all his action would be forever guided by Christian notions of charity and sacrifice.

As the priest led us through our vows, surrounded by many witnesses, I vowed to myself to deny my lord nothing. At that time of my innocence, I could not foresee that my desire might ever be contrary to his.

Before our wedding mass, I scarcely noticed the large company of our guests, which included the very King of all England, Uther Pendragon. His nut-brown beard showed no trace of silver, and he appeared jolly and strong enough to bear the weight of a jewel-encrusted gold crown without finding it wearisome. He was surrounded by attendants in livery, all adorned with the sign of the dragon. The King had no wife, but there was no shortage of fair women in his entourage.

I had heard that the King traveled with a mighty sorcerer named Merlin, but in all the royal company, I could not tell who that might be.

The wedding feast was more elaborate than any I had seen. We were served every bird that could be eaten, from doves to pheasants to geese, with good roast venison to follow. A course of sweets honored the sweetness of the occasion. There were minstrels, lute players, jugglers, and jesters.

And then came the time for dancing. As the musicians played the first notes, I leapt to my feet and held out my hands to my wedded lord, thinking that none but he could join me in the first dance of the evening. As I did so, most of the assembled company rose and took their places.

Geoffrey stood up, but he did so only to acknowledge the approach of King Uther, who strode to me, held out both his hands, and then wrapped me in his arms, whispering "Igraine! Be not afraid of me."

The closeness of the King, who was clearly a man like all others, alarmed me despite his message of encouragement. I felt myself growing hot beneath my clothes, and then the whispering assaulted my ears. The whole company seemed to be repeating: "*Jus primae noctis.*"

Impulsively, I looked toward my parents, and saw them both smiling and nodding at me, as if to bid me accept the King's attention. Then I looked at my newly wedded lord, who gazed meaningfully at me and at the man who held me so possessively.

Clearly, Geoffrey had already made an agreement with King Uther to grant him the right to deflower his bride in exchange for a feudal alliance. My maidenhead was the price to be paid for the King's protection of the Duchy of Cornwall against any who might seek to invade and overthrow my lord's rule.

I knew that King Uther wished to unite all Britain under the sign of the dragon and to offer peace to all those who followed him while threatening war against all who might seek to overthrow him. The marriage that Geoffrey had negotiated with my parents was part of a strategy to keep us all safe.

My husband and my father clearly feared that their armies would be no match for the army of the King, and therefore they had united to offer him my body for one night. Despite my lord's claim to revere the sanctity of a marriage between one man and one woman, ordained by God, his need for the King's good will trumped all.

Why did I not foresee what would happen on my wedding night? I had been thinking like a child.

My despair must have shown on my face. King Uther released me, but retained one of my small hands in the heat of his larger one. "My lady!" he whispered. "We are being observed. Please do not refuse me openly, and I will not violate you against your will."

The King's assurance restored me to something resembling my former state of calm, even if I could never again be a light-hearted maid. "Your Majesty," I responded, looking into his eyes to judge of his sincerity, then down at the floor to appear modest.

The whole assemblage seemed to sigh with relief when the King led me in the dance, and all those standing began to move together. Geoffrey chose one of my bridesmaids as his dancing partner, and she looked pleased enough.

The roomful of bodies, all swaying and whirling in rhythm, reminded me of the waves of the sea beyond our walls. *Even the King,* I thought, *cannot foresee or control everything that will happen in the world.*

Too soon, the time for dancing was over—or at least, no one intended to continue dancing in all their finery. Geoffrey embraced me and kissed me on the lips, as though seeking forgiveness, and promised that he would welcome me back the following morning.

"Please bear it for my sake, Igraine," he begged. "I will love you dearly for your sacrifice, and I will always honor you as my faithful wife after this night."

"You might have warned me," I responded. "You make it difficult for me to trust you, my lord." I turned toward the King, who was waiting to escort me to a bedchamber on an upper floor of the castle. The King was in good humor, and he wrapped a strong arm about my slender waist with an air of familiarity.

I could go mad, thought I. No, I amended to myself: *I could feign madness.* I could wrest the circlet off my hair and tear the leaves and flowers to pieces before trampling them underfoot. I would be deflowered indeed, and I could tear my gown to shreds, screaming curses at all who had planned my humiliation.

I could run, and if I could exit the doors of the castle without being captured, I could throw myself off a cliff into the dark, surging sea, watched by the uncaring stars above me. I could gasp for breath, feeling my mouth and lungs filling with cold brine. I could die painfully, knowing that Geoffrey would be tormented by a fantasy of me in Hell, condemned to suffer there for eternity as a self-murderess.

I had not the will to carry out this plan. While imagining myself running, running, down stone corridors and into the night air, I was walking up an endless staircase, guided by the King's arm and his discreet whispering in my ear. "My lady," he told me, "I have a man's desire, but I have no wish to break your spirit. Please believe that I wish to earn your trust, not your hatred."

A fragrance arose from the King's strong limbs, from his beard and his hair and his very breath. It was the smell of a man, but as sweet as the hedges in spring. I sensed no disdain in him, and no wish to treat me as a captive maiden taken in war. The air surrounding him seemed to vibrate with his joyful spirit.

I was perplexed. I had not expected to find such delight in his company.

The King guided me into the bedchamber before him. I could feel his warm breath on my neck.

The bed rose before me, draped with a soft coverlet and pillows stuffed with goose down. Had I been alone, I would have locked the door, undone my laces, stripped off every stitch of my clothing, and lain down at ease.

"Igraine, my dear, you are no court lady, and for that I am grateful." He turned me to face him, and wrapped his arms about me. He pressed his lips to mine, and I felt as if I could melt.

"Little white swan," he said, laughing into my eyes. He held me by the waist and raised me off the ground. "Your weight is like feathers, but you are no light wench." He smiled at his own wit. I was relieved that he did not consider me a whore. He kissed my chin and tipped it upward so that he could leave a trail of hot kisses along my neck and down to my bodice.

The King's breathing increased until it sounded like wind in my ears, and my own kept pace with his. I felt lightheaded. I wrapped my arms round his back to hold myself steady, and this

seemed to please him beyond words. "Lady, you would tempt a
hermit in his cell." The King's voice seemed to stroke the skin
under my clothes and resonate in my very head.

I could feel myself trembling, and a certain tingling
throughout my lower parts reminded me that my desire matched
his, regardless of my intentions. He was more than the King of
England. He was the man who had courted me in dreams so secret
that I had never confided them to anyone.

With one arm about my waist, King Uther pressed my
backside against him. I could feel the hardness of his cock pressing
through his snug breeches and my gown. Oh, how I wished to
feel that marble scepter pushing in between my legs as deeply as
it could go!

I pulled his arm away, and he did not hinder me. I turned to
face him. "My Lord, if you think so, why have you never said so
before my wedding to another?"

"Please forgive my hesitation, my lady," he said, smiling, "but I
esteem your parents greatly, and you have not been long out of
childhood. I did not wish to offend them by courting you too soon."

I could not think of an answer to this. What if King Uther had
made me his Queen before the Duke of Cornwall had reached an
agreement with my parents? I would not now feel like a traitor to
my wedded lord.

"Alas!" continued the King. He pulled me into his embrace,
and I did not resist. "Now I can only claim you for one night, if
you will have me. Igraine, will you deny me that?"

Tears burned my eyelids. The King's skin was hot and moist
where it touched me, and mine felt the same. My breasts wished
to be squeezed and suckled. The tingling between my thighs
prompted me to move my hips as though in the lascivious dance
of a Saracen concubine.

I no longer wondered how I could bear to feel the King's eyes
and his hands on my naked body, and to feel his cock claiming
me. I wondered how I could give him up.

Geoffrey expected me to return to him with my maidenhead truly lost, and he would be pleased. How could that be? I had seen him gaze at the King as a sunflower lifts its petals to the sun. A Christian man could hardly offer himself to a man he admired without fearing the flames of Hell, but he could secretly dream of such pleasures, and he could offer his bride as a valuable gift. I resolved to consider the complexity of our three-sided alliance when I could be alone with my thoughts.

King Uther held me to his broad bosom and kissed me passionately. "Dear heart," he asked tenderly, "are you afraid?"

I considered my answer. "Not of you, my lord." I resolved not to complain if his weapon felt too large in my scabbard, and I hoped that any pain he might cause would be as brief as a flash of lightning. My heart pounded within my ribs as they rose and fell with my breath.

The King gently removed my circlet and released my hair to flow over my shoulders. He sighed almost inaudibly as he buried his nose in my loose tresses. "Fair she-knight in the trials of love," he laughed. I knew that he did not intend any discourtesy.

He explored my gown to find ways to remove it from me, but he was clearly no lady's-maid. I couldn't help smiling as I helped by untying my laces and by pulling my garments over my head.

The King obliged me by removing his tunic and breeches as I assisted as much as I could.

We lay together on the bed, wrapped in each other's arms, inhaling each other's breath. He kissed me from my neck to my shoulders to the tips of my breasts. With his tongue, he coaxed their tips to grow stiff, and when I thought I would faint from pleasure, he pulled each one into his mouth and suckled me like a nursing babe. I writhed against him.

King Uther gently spread my thighs apart. He stroked between the lips of my cleft until my moisture increased, and I could see it on his finger. "Igraine," said he, "do you give pleasure to yourself?"

"No," I answered quickly, fearing to be scorned if I answered truthfully. "Pleasure myself! I do not know how."

The King's cock was as upright as the oaken mast of a ship. Despite my eagerness, its size alarmed me. "Are you sure, my dear?" he smiled. "I would greatly enjoy watching you try."

"My lord! Do you command me to deflower myself?" Even while I showed my astonishment, I could see the wisdom of his plan, if such it was.

"Igraine, my dearest," he answered patiently, "I will not proceed without your full will. I cannot. You must show me what you desire."

That was not a simple thing. Had he left the room, I would have stroked my private parts with abandon until I brought myself to a shivering ecstasy, unseen by any.

"Perhaps," added the King slyly, "a lady of your parents' court has shown you how pleasure may be shared among women."

Perhaps indeed, but why would a King desire such knowledge? I considered his word, *cannot*. I thought of his magical advisor, Merlin, and wondered if the King were under a spell that would bring him grievous harm if he ever ravished a woman, even one resigned to suffer such indignity from her King.

Just as he could go no further without my heartfelt consent, I could not deny myself relief. Without another word, I withdrew from the King, lay on my side, and pulled my knees toward my belly. I glanced at him and slipped one of my hands between the hairy lips, now wet with dew, between my thighs. I closed my eyes to shut out the sight of his piqued expression.

I found the little knot of flesh at the head of my opening, and it was almost unbearably tender. I caressed it until my inner flesh demanded attention, and then I pushed my finger as far into my cleft as it would go. My lower mouth seemed to open within, as though hungry for meat, and so I offered it another finger, and that one was thicker.

I used my two fingers to push in and out of my secret cave, and my rhythm increased from a walk to a gallop

"So that is how you dance a measure," remarked the King, barely containing his mirth. He lay behind me so as to hold me fast and press his hard cock against my backside. "Allow me," he said, and replaced my two fingers with one of his own. I grew so excited that he was able to enter me with two of his fingers, although his were altogether different from mine, being larger in every dimension as well as more insistent.

My ecstasy approached, and I feared appearing to the King as a madwoman or a she-beast. "My lord!" I said quietly.

"My love," he answered as warmly as a thought. "Show me your pleasure."

His use of my name as he explored my inner flesh so intimately sent me into a frenzy, and I could not control my response. "Ah!" I gasped, as my cleft sought to hold and keep him within. My dew became so copious that I was sure I would leave a wet stain on the bed-covering.

King Uther withdrew his fingers, rolled me in his arms, and kissed me as though he never wished his lips to be parted from mine. His tongue even found its way into my mouth and greeted my own. "Good wench," he teased. "Did you find it sweet to surrender?"

"Yes," I confessed under my breath.

The King seized my fingers and wrapped them round his solid cock. I soon learned from him how he wished to be stroked, and I continued this service until the mouth of his organ spewed forth its own dew in a fountain, accompanied by a long groan from the King's throat.

When he had regained enough breath to speak, he said, "Igraine! You are the mistress of my heart."

I was not certain whether I had yet been deflowered according to custom. The King settled my uncertainty by settling himself atop me, supported on his elbows. He showed me how to spread my legs apart as widely as possible so that he would have a clear shot at his target. He guided the head of his cock into my wet cleft, and it found lodging there.

To my great relief, I felt nothing but joy. This state did not last, however.

In a series of heaves, the King pushed his cock deeper and deeper into me, and it caused such a variety of sensations that I hardly knew how to respond. There were sharp pains like pricks from a needle, accompanied by a steady ache and the tingling of pleasure like the ringing of a silver bell over the thump of a drum.

When the King was lodged as deeply into me as he could be, he continued moving up and down until, with a groan like that of a dying warrior, he stopped. I could feel something twitching deep within me, and his cock brought forth a response from me, like an echo of the paroxysms I had felt when his fingers had stroked me so well.

His cock softened enough that it could be withdrawn, but my lord—my lover—continued to lie atop me, resting his weight on the bedding rather than on me. I could feel our combined love-fluid trickling under my thighs. The hair of his body was like the warm pelt of a wolf over my breasts, and his beard tickled my face. I felt as if I could erupt into ecstasy again and again, simply from his nearness.

I could not refrain from twisting away from the King to see whether any trace of blood, the sure sign of my deflowering, could be seen on the bed-covering. It was there.

"My dearest love," whispered the King, "you are yet unsatisfied."

"No, my lord," I assured him. "For the moment, I am perfectly content."

"Igraine," he told me as though divulging a secret, "you will bear the heir to my throne."

"I certainly will not," I told him. "Forgive me, my lord, but have you forgotten that I am not your wife? Any child I might bear to you would be a royal bastard, and nothing more."

"Call me Uther," he commanded. "I will not have you address me as your lord when we have been so closely joined. We cannot be parted now."

But we must, thought I, *or dire consequences shall follow.*

"My lord Uther," I protested. "I have a duty to my husband,

the Duke of Cornwall. He bears the utmost loyalty to you, his King, and he—he lives according to his faith. As a Christian, he would not share me with another man beyond this night."

I did not dare tell Uther what I knew: that Geoffrey would gladly lie with the King himself, but he would not simply give up his new wife and accept abandonment by both of us. No gentleman of rank could be expected to accept such discourtesy without protest.

King Uther caressed my back as though offering me comfort. "If that man is his King," he explained, "your husband will have no choice."

A powerful wizard, I thought, and only he, could enable all three of us to have our hearts' desire. And if there is no spell to meet such a requirement, all our hearts may well be broken.

"Uther," I pleaded. "If you wish me to address you so, hear this. If you break the bargain you made with my wedded lord, you will break the peace of your kingdom. I would rather throw myself into the sea than become known to all as another Helena of Troy, a cause of hellish war among men."

The King tightened his embrace, as though to claim me as his. "Igraine," he said, "calm yourself. I will never let you come to harm. I shall invite the Duke of Cornwall and yourself to visit me in a fortnight, and I shall ask my counselors for advice on this matter. You have no cause for fear."

A King can be wrong, and many past wars have proven so beyond a doubt. Yet I could not refuse the prospect of visiting him in his own abode.

As daylight spread throughout the sky, we both rose and dressed ourselves. The servants had wisely respected our privacy, but when we emerged together into a corridor, they greeted us both with the smiles of conspirators.

"My lady," said a maid in my husband's service, "may I offer you assistance?" She gazed directly at my hair, which I had plaited in haste to make myself fit to be seen in company.

Servants and minor nobles bustled to and fro, curtseying and bowing to the King and looking at me with veiled amusement. I needed no words of advice to inform me that from that day forward, I was to present myself as the Duchess of Cornwall, highest lady of the household, and a jewel on my husband's breastplate. Igraine the untamed colt was to be banished.

"Yes," I told the maid, as though my state of disarray were her fault. "Please excuse me, my lord," I told the King. He smiled indulgently as the maid led me to a room that seemed to exist only for the attiring of ladies.

When I was ready, Geoffrey was telling the King: "You honor us, my liege." In a different tone, he said, "My dear lady wife," and seized me by the hands. If I flinched at his touch, he disdained to take note of it.

As the King's attendants prepared him for departure, he would not allow me to leave his sight. "I shall gladly await your arrival in London, my lord and my lady," said the King, "where I shall repay your hospitality in full."

No one could mistake his meaning. Geoffrey gazed earnestly at his lord, but at length the light faded from his eyes. He wore an expression of pain as he bid the King godspeed. I could not refuse the King's embrace, nor his kiss, and how they heartened me! Nonetheless, I received them like a condemned prisoner receiving last rites before an appointment with death.

That night, Geoffrey bedded me tenderly. As I lay in his arms, he asked me whether I still felt sore, and whether I had pleased the King. "Throughout the long night," asked my wedded lord, as though thinking aloud, "did he speak of me?"

"Indeed he did," I answered. "He told me that he holds you in the esteem of an older brother who gives wise counsel." Geoffrey seemed so gratified that I continued as recklessly as I had begun. "He said that Cornwall is the anchor of Britain, but he asked me not to reveal the importance of our duchy to anyone beyond its borders."

Geoffrey entered me with the eagerness of a man who drinks from the Fountain of Youth. My hunger had been awakened on the previous night, and I met his passion with my own, although mine was perhaps closer to the passion of a martyr than was his. The pleasure of our honeymoon would not last long, and this I knew.

A fortnight later, we traveled to London with a small retinue. On our arrival, the King's attendants took charge of our steeds and led them away.

King Uther himself strode into the courtyard to greet us. He kissed me fondly, seized me in his arms, and lifted me from the paving-stones.

I feared revealing how much I enjoyed this reunion. "My lord!" I cried. Alas, my response was ill considered.

"Welcome, welcome!" exclaimed the King, still holding me in his arms. "Cornwall, we trust that you had a safe journey."

This was the greeting of any host to a guest for whom he feels no particular affection. I could see the hurt in Geoffrey's eyes, and his awareness that his hidden love for the King might never be requited, nor yet be replaced by the love of another.

And still, Uther would not let me go, despite my efforts to slip from his arms. He seemed to wish all the world to know how he regarded me.

My husband grasped the hilt of his sword. "Sir," he said calmly. "Please release the Duchess, my wife. Such familiarity is unseemly."

"Cornwall, my brother!" shouted the King, making no effort to avoid being heard by all who surrounded us. "The lady is a treasure, and you have given her to us. We are grateful, and if you remain loyal, you shall be rewarded. Do not test the patience of your King now by making impertinent demands."

Shock, sorrow, and outrage competed in Geoffrey's face. "Sir!" shouted the Duke, pulling his sword free. "Release my wife at once!"

"My lords!" I responded. I strove to control my voice as my feet returned to the ground. "I beg you to put up your weapons. As I owe allegiance to you both, you must show courtesy to each other."

Geoffrey did not move, nor did King Uther. "Do you threaten us, sir?" The King was immediately surrounded by archers with drawn bows, his personal guard.

"Peace!" I screamed. I probably sounded more like a falcon than like a noblewoman. "For the love of all that's holy!"

Geoffrey brandished his sword as though he intended to kill or to die for my honor. "My wife is a Christian lady!" he declared.

"She is not to be traded like a common whore."

"Your Majesty," I said, "we must take our leave. I implore you to excuse us." A small group of the King's men surrounded me. "Our Savior loved his fellows," I admonished the general company. "He commanded us to do the same. We will not disturb the peace of the King."

Holding my skirts, I slipped between two guardsmen and ran to find the royal stables and mount a horse before I could be prevented. My husband sensibly returned his sword to his scabbard and followed me, while a half-dozen of our attendants accompanied us.

Geoffrey dressed and mounted his horse, Heavenly Grace, with a dexterity born of long practice, and helped me to climb up behind him. Grace's hooves struck sparks from the stones as the faithful steed bore us beyond the castle gates.

A great clamor behind us caused me to turn my head to see a confusion of fists and steel. Several of our men, wearing the device of Cornish choughs, fought in deadly earnest with the King's men in their dragon livery. I grieved to see it, but we could not remain to offer help to our loyal defenders.

We were able to give rest and sustenance to Grace in my parents' stables, and they offered us a fresh horse for the remainder of our journey. We had scarcely arrived home at Castle Tintagel when Geoffrey bid me remain there while he gathered a fighting force to accompany him to Castle Terrabel, which he intended to defend from the King's men. We both feared that the King would declare the Duke of Cornwall a traitor, and his lands forfeit.

Geoffrey begged of me a handkerchief, laden with my scent, to carry with him always. He said it would give him courage in the trial to come.

I have waited alone for a fortnight, and no messenger has brought me news of good or ill. I scarcely know what news would cheer me.

The priest, Father Blanchemains, assures me daily that God favors the virtuous man, and in this war, my husband surely has a host of angels on his side. The Father tells me often that Geoffrey was chosen to defeat licentiousness, as embodied by the King, and idolatry, as practiced by godless pagans and Saracens.

Although I am assured that God has set his plan, I am exhorted to daily prayer. I pray only that I not be with child by any man.

Here ends the first part of my tale. There is much more to tell, as you shall see.

The tedium of my days ended when a lone man in armor appeared at our gates. I wondered what horseless knight would seek lodging here, and whom he served.

"Where is my wife, the Duchess?" A merry voice rang through the hall even as a servant-boy ran to tell me that the Duke had returned from the siege of Castle Terrabel.

The man stood in the hall, holding his helmet. He wore the sun-browned face of Geoffrey, but with an expression altogether new for him. He had my husband's voice, but it filled the space and reverberated from the walls in a way that Geoffrey's never did.

There was a glamor on the knight. To put on the face and body and the very voice of another is the work of the Devil, or so my husband would say. There was even a smell in the air that was not there before: the scent of sorcery. I approached slowly, observing the man as closely as I could.

He demanded acknowledgment. "My dearest love, are you not filled with joy that I am alive?"

Yes! I thought. *Praise to all the gods that brought you safe to me.* I ran to him and touched his nut-brown beard. "Yes, my lord!" I assured him. "But you are changed." There was no mistaking the gleam in those blue-grey eyes. My husband Geoffrey's were warm and brown.

"Ah, you will not embrace me while I am clad in armor," said he. "That can soon be remedied. Boy!" Three attendants came to remove their master's armor, piece by piece, and carried it away to be tended. Perhaps the foolish lads then told each other tales of how many arrows that armor had resisted, and how brave was the man who wore it.

The man with Geoffrey's face wore only a plain tunic and breeches. He held me by the shoulders and kissed me as though asking a question. "I have longed for you, Igraine."

Tears filled my eyes. "I have longed to see you whole and strong, my lord," I answered, and this was true no matter who stood before me. Only one of them, however, required my wholehearted consent before he could touch me. I threw my arms round him and repaid his kiss. Even if Satan awaited me in Hell, I could not resist the temptation that stood before me.

The man swept me into his arms and pressed me against his coarse tunic. I could hear his heart beating beneath it. "Geoffrey," I said quietly, for his ears alone. "Have you slain the King that you love dearly?"

I felt a wavering in the arms of the man who held me. "Lady," he said faintly, "let us be merry this day. We may speak of slaying another time."

"We may indeed," I told him. "And we may speak of Merlin, the great sorcerer, and of treachery and deception."

The man lifted me in his arms and strode to the staircase. "Lady, this is a conversation for our ears alone. If you please, we shall continue it in our bedchamber."

I could have protested, but in truth, my awakened skin and all my womanly parts had been neglected during the time of my waiting, and I wanted to be well pleased. The man released me before the door to our bedchamber, and I opened it to invite him in.

He responded by smacking my backside through my skirt. "Oh, wife," said he, "There is no woman like you."

Wife! I repeated soundlessly to myself. From my lover's mouth, that word was sweeter than honey.

"Perhaps," I said aloud, "but there is a confounding resemblance here. My lord, if I am to receive you as you wish, I have a right to know whether I am committing a sin or doing my duty. No man has a right to take me by deceit."

In the slant of light from the lead-paned window, the man

glowed with merriment. "Igraine," he said, smiling, "I shall show you that which is different for every man alive." He removed his clothing and stood before me as naked as a babe. The brown hair grew plentiful as ever on his chest, and a matching pelt graced his cock, which rose with every breath he took. "Would you kiss it, dear lady?" he teased.

I knelt to hold it in both my hands, and stroked it to its fullest length. I touched its head lightly with my lips, and the man pushed forward with his whole groin. I surmised what he wished me do, and I guided his cock into my mouth, inch by inch.

"My dearest love," he groaned. "You are kissing the little man who cannot lie, and I shall presently give you the proof."

I used my tongue and my teeth on his shaft, while my fingers played on the sacks of flesh below, as though I were squeezing air out of the bagpipes. His cock jerked as I discovered different ways to summon a response. At once, fluid gushed from him and filled my mouth with a briny flavor. I regretted never having tasted such liquor before. I sensed that every man's essence must be different, but I lacked experience to distinguish one from another.

"You are Venus herself," said my grateful companion, "a mistress of the arts of love. You shall be rewarded."

He helped me out of my clothing and turned me about so that he could admire me from every angle, as though he had never done so before. He kissed a trail from my neck to each breast, down my belly and into the moist hair between my legs. I could smell my own fragrance.

"My lady," he asked, "will you bend over the bed that I may offer my tribute from behind?"

I did as he asked, and he squeezed my buttocks as though their shape delighted him. He tickled me until I shook with laughter, and then he opened my cleft and pushed his cock inside. I felt too weak to retain my footing on the floor, but he held me in place.

I felt as if I could explode with pleasure. This time, he continued until I feared that he would weary of the dance before I would.

The man who pressed himself so eagerly into my depths reached beneath me with one hand. On one finger he wore a jeweled ring, and he used this so cleverly to stroke my little nubbin so that I shivered in ecstasy and drenched the bed-covering with my dew.

Afterward, we lay together to kiss, caress, and play at other games. "Igraine," said my companion, "what if you are with child? Would you hate me for it?"

"Neither the father nor the child," I assured him. "I can probably bear the torments of birth as well as any woman, but I would grieve to think that any other has suffered so that our love could flower."

"Dear heart," he said, stroking my hair as it lay about my head. "I have commanded that none be harmed for our sake."

"That is well," I replied, "because the King ought to know of the love that Geoffrey of Cornwall bears for him. Anyone with eyes can see that it is far beyond the duty of a subject, and there is no shame in it."

The man beside me tried to kiss the worry from my forehead. "You trouble yourself too much, Igraine," he protested. "We have not spoken of shame."

"Have you not charged my lord Cornwall with treason?" I replied. "If a loyal subject be forced to act the role of a traitor to the King he adores, who then has broken faith?" Tears spilled from my eyes, and I wept for us all three.

The man's eyes darkened like the sky when a storm approaches. Before my blurred sight, the features of my husband Geoffrey wavered and resolved into those of Uther, my beloved. "What would you have me do, woman?" he demanded. "I know something of the love of soldiers, men who face death on the battlefield, and know that each night they spend together might be their last. Cornwall the Pious was not the first to offer me his body without saying a word. Was I obliged to answer him?" He paused to wipe away my tears. "Little bird, you cannot imagine the life of a King. If I am to control a kingdom, I cannot play Zeus to every shepherd who wishes to be carried away to Mount Olympus."

"Yet you would carry me away." I could not reproach him for it.

"I would," he smiled. "I know not why, but you please me better than the comeliest youth I ever trained to swing a sword."

Uther seemed determined to dispel my sorrow and my fears with ribaldry. "Igraine, if you are wise in the ways of men with men, would it please you to serve as my squire this night?" He grasped my arm above the elbow and squeezed gently, as though testing my muscles. He did the same to my other arm, and his expression provoked me to laugh through my tears. "A fine lad you are, Alan," he said. "You shall make a worthy bedfellow."

The man raised me until I sat upright. He embraced me from behind, and held my breasts in his two hands. "The bosom of a warrior," he remarked, pinching my nipples, "in the fullness of time, of course." He stretched one hand downward to the hair that covered my opening. "You lack something of a man, Alan, but no matter."

"My lord," I responded in the spirit of the game, "I regret falling short of your expectations."

"Well, allow me to continue my inspection, and perhaps we will each find compensations in the other. Lie on your belly, lad."

I did as the King commanded, and he pressed a slow, firm hand down my back to the cleft of my buttocks. He kneaded each globe as though it were dough for bread, and smacked each in turn. The skin of my backside had not received such attention since I was a child.

"Have I displeased you, my lord?" I asked.

"Not at all, good boy," he answered. "I am merely testing your mettle."

Uther proceeded to seek out my smaller hole with a gentle finger, but I was as uneasy as a young man at the mercy of his master. "An unopened rosebud," said he. "The maidenhead of a youth. I shall treat it with care."

At first, I dreaded being violated in that foulest of regions, but the slow, circular penetration of Uther's finger banished my dread completely. "Just a thimbleful of fat would be a magical balm for our purpose, Alan, but we are poorly supplied. Will you allow me to have my will without it?"

"My liege," I answered. "I am your faithful servant, but will you allow me to decline?"

"Alan," he muttered, as I turned my head to see his face. "You know not what you ask."

"Indeed, I know not," I retorted. "Please enlighten me, my lord." I sat to hear his reply.

"Alan, you must learn from my example." He pushed me back onto my belly, and smacked my bottom. "War inspires the noblest of knights to the vile use of ladies. I have long wished to unite all England that it may be strengthened, and with my army, I have overrun many a castle and a town. Ten years since, when my men and I were in the north, we sought out all the wenches in a poor village, little thinking to find a powerful sorceress there. But such she was, and she took such offense at being ravished that she cursed me to death, should I ever again offer such mistreatment to any being, even if it were a sheep."

I hoped that Uther could see my smile. "She did well, "I remarked. "She was a northern wise-woman indeed. I hope she spread that curse amongst all your men."

A heavy sigh blew through my hair like wind. "She did, lad, and although we were a small company, we have become noted for our chivalry since that day, even beyond Britain. I cannot bed anyone I cannot seduce, and the willingness of my companion must be strong enough to break the spell that would visit my own violence on my own head."

"Uther," I asked, "could not Merlin undo that spell?"

"Ah," replied the King, resting a hand on my bottom. "I have no doubt, but to what purpose? No, my boy, I have come to accept the condition in which I must live. Love must not be forced, and who better to embody that principle than a leader of men? I deserve no release from the spell, nor do I seek it."

My heart was moved, but my loins still craved attention. I wriggled beneath my lover's hand. "Please, my lord," I begged, "mightn't you find a thimbleful of fat in the kitchen below?"

He laughed heartily. "Better than that, Alan," he told me. "I misled you to find out your will. I carry an unguent with me." He proceeded to coat two fingers liberally in a lubricant, which then eased their way, one at a time, so deeply into me that the sparks of pleasure ignited my larger opening.

He stroked and explored that part of me which had never known such an intrusion, even from my own hands, and it brought me to ecstasy beyond my imagining. "Oh!" I screamed, then quickly covered my mouth with a handful of the coverlet.

"My dear lad," he whispered, "how do you like the games of man with man? Shall I take your bottom with a better weapon?"

I was so aroused in my cunt, and so afraid of spoiling my pleasure with unwanted pain, that I reluctantly refused him. "Please, dear master," I replied, "I prefer to offer you that when next we meet for the games of love. Would you enter me by a larger entrance?"

Uther laughed, rolled me about in his arms, and plunged into me without further ado. I wrapped my legs around his waist, and clung to him as his own bottom rose and fell with his thrusts. We galloped together to a most satisfying conclusion.

We were both so indiscreet in our noisemaking that I feared discovery by the servants; luckily, we were not disturbed by approaching footsteps. We lay panting in each other's arms until, as though returning from the land of Faery, we each became aware of where we were. And then we embraced in earnest, wishing to postpone the intrusion of grim reality.

We fell into the sweetest sleep imaginable, but my dreams were troubled by the image of a lost knight in armor, calling for my help as he strove in vain to swim in the merciless sea.

On the morrow, we awoke to the light of truth. King Uther sat beside me, usurping Geoffrey's bed. "Igraine, if you are a true follower of Christ Jesus," said my lover, "you are bound to forgive me, are you not?"

I laughed. "I am no true Christian, but I forgive you anyway, my love," I told him. "Perhaps it is I who need forgiveness."

The King feigned surprise. "You are the most blameless

woman in England," he said, "but if you crave my pardon, you may certainly have it."

I resolved to ask Father Blanchmains, and then Lord Merlin, whether a sinner may pardon his fellow-conspirator in sin.

We arose from bed, of course, because we had much to do. When I summoned Hilda, my maid, to dress my hair and fetch my attire for the day, I asked her to bring me a gown as brown as the earth because I expected doleful news.

In the afternoon, when the sun was highest, a troupe of men in dragon livery brought Geoffrey to Castle Tintagel on a litter. I rushed to see my husband, and to offer him my care, but it was too late. His face was cold where I touched it, and no breath moved his still form. A horrible wound in his side showed too clearly what had robbed him of life, and all his bearers were smeared with his blood.

King Uther grew pale at the sight of his adversary. "My lord," I demanded, "what say you to this?"

"I swear on my mother's life, Igraine," he answered, "I gave no command for him to be slain. I wished for him to be captured only, and for his lands to be forfeit to the crown."

To the astonishment of our attendants, the King fell to his knees and pressed his lips to the pale forehead of my husband's corpse.

The King soon recovered his composure, rose to his feet, and commanded his men to give him a full account of the battle. One of his captains confessed that the Duke of Cornwall had surprised them as they approached Castle Terrabel, where they supposed he was prepared to wait out a siege. The Duke's men, said the captain, attacked first and with the fury of those who believe they must right an unforgivable wrong.

"We are soldiers," the captain told his King. "We were forced to fight for our lives." His explanation held a dismal logic, and I could hardly find him more villainous than any other man in his profession.

I asked Father Blanchmains to help me arrange a suitable funeral for my late lord. There was much weeping in the castle that day, for my lord had been kind to his servants. I hoped with all my heart that

Geoffrey's spirit was at peace, and that he was reunited with his first wife, a most pious lady whom he had loved dearly.

At length, King Uther was compelled to return to his court in London, while I was allowed to remain in Castle Tintagel for the time being, where I could be seen to live simply in my widowhood, and to stand on a cliff to hear the sea's lullaby.

When I had been in mourning three months, the shape of my belly showed to all what I had known in my heart for weeks past: I was with child. I sent a messenger to London to inform the King, although it seemed likely to me that Merlin had observed me in a scrying glass.

The King returned to me post-haste. In privacy, he delighted in pressing his ear to my round belly to hear the heartbeat of the dear babe growing within me. "If he is a son, I wish him to be named Arthur," said he, "an eagle among men and future King of all Britain."

"How so, my lord Uther?" I asked. "I am no more than your mistress, and I was married to the Duke of Cornwall, whom you have deemed a traitor, when the babe was conceived. Our poor child is more likely to be murdered or driven into exile than hailed as your son and heir. Should you declare him so, your nobles will surely rise up against you."

King Uther held me on his lap, with my head on his shoulder. He did not seem discouraged. "Igraine, my dear, you are as wise as you are fair, but my men will bear witness that your husband was slain before our son was conceived. Merlin himself will confess in public to his role in my deception of you."

I laughed. "A poor deception, Uther," I told him. "Perhaps Merlin needs to practice his art more diligently."

"Perhaps," the King answered mildly. "And as for the skeptics in my court, nothing softens opposition so well as a grand celebration. The streets of London will run with wine for our wedding."

"There can be no wedding," I reproved him, "if there has been no proposal."

"My lady, I beg you to accept my offer." He buried his face in my hair. "Our people will love you better as Queen than ever they have loved a sinful King."

"I accept!" I laughed. "Dear heart, I still fear that our son may not be accepted by all."

"Then I will charge Merlin to devise a sign to prove our son's royal blood to all who doubt it. If anything can sway the crowd more than a procession and a holiday for every butcher, soldier, and apprentice, it is a display of divine right."

And so it was with our handsome and clever son Arthur, when he was as young and untamed as I had been when first compelled to accept my fate. But that is a tale for another time.

Questing
Charles Payseur

Lancelot ran the streets of Chicago, laughter rising up in the air like a standard, proclaiming him to the world. His arms were outstretched, his eyes closed, his long blond hair trailing behind him. Around him people swore, saw him as just another dumb tourist, but he didn't care. Why would he? He was in Chicago a full day ahead of schedule.

He didn't need to be. He was so far ahead in points that none of the others had much hope of ever catching up, even if he took a holiday. Instead he pushed further ahead, lost himself in the simple pleasure of the game and of winning the game. What else was there to do with immortality? Jousting was now only done at Renaissance Festivals, and he wouldn't be caught dead in such a place. Why live in the past when the present had so much to offer? For Lancelot, there was only the game, the quests. And whenever he felt the weight of centuries pushing down on him, the boredom, the tired ache, he reminded himself that he was Lancelot, the greatest knight in the world, and he kept right on going.

"I don't see why you're so happy," a voice said, trailing him, and Lancelot stopped cold, eyes flying open. More curses erupted at his sudden halt, but a soft chuckle pierced them all. Palomides. Dark skin and amused grin and deep brown eyes. His hair was cut short these days, a small goatee trimmed thin and sharp on his face. Tall and fit, the man walked toward Lancelot with a muted grace and almost lazy energy.

"Just because you recovered the day you lost in Nevada?" Palomides continued. "Did you think that anyone would really believe you had gone all the way south to New Orleans to catch a boat to Africa? As if you'd ever miss the chance to go north through France."

Lancelot frowned, though the emotion didn't reach his eyes.

Any complication was a good thing, after all, any distraction welcome. Especially from Palomides, though most of the time the man kept his distance. Lancelot had a reputation among the knights, and after a half dozen fiery affairs and lovers' spats spanning continents, none seemed willing to let themselves get drawn close. Not that Lancelot lacked in romantic partners. With a whole world of men and women out there to win, he kept himself busy. Still, his eyes wandering up Palomides' body, he couldn't help but feel he had missed out on something.

"I suppose the others are around as well, then?" he asked. "Lamorak going to jump out next? Or Percival? Lionel?" But Palomides was shaking his head.

Lancelot smiled. Things were always more interesting one-on-one.

"They're all at least a day behind, probably more. They caught a quest on their way through Texas, and you know the rules."

The rules. As in the rules of the game. The game they'd been playing to stay sane the last few centuries. They had to do something, after all, being immortal. Otherwise they'd probably end up going mad and keeping the old hatreds alive, like Tristan had, or Gawaine, or any of the others caught in the past. Not him. Lancelot looked at the curse of the Grail somewhat differently, which is to say not as a curse at all. Oh, the first time it was a surprise, to close his eyes in final sleep and then open them up again as a child. Reincarnation, some said, but it hardly mattered. He'd gotten quite good at it, was able to always set money aside for his next self to find later. Enough to finance the game. It was always difficult the first few years of each new life, so full of knowledge and memories and unable to do anything about it. They had to act like Ricky or Ferdinand or whatever their new parents named them and blend in until they were old enough to play the game. But they remained the same in spirit. Lancelot was always Lancelot in his own mind. And he normally left home early. He had never liked being subject to anyone else's control. He didn't like to be tied down. He wanted freedom, adventure. Even after so many centuries he was still living for that next excitement.

"Well hurrah for us, then," Lancelot said, trying to figure out Palomides' move. Was he trying to lure Lancelot into a trap, or was it something else? Lancelot decided to come on strong. "Care to slip away and find a room or something?"

Palomides gave a small laugh and adopted an infuriatingly adorable smile, just the corners of his mouth curling up. He had a secret.

"Is their quest through Texas worth a lot of points or something?" Not that it would matter, with the lead that Lancelot had over most of the others. Only Palomides was even close.

"Not as much as the one a little north of here right now." Just like Palomides, to be thinking of business first. Even in their first lives, Palomides the Questing Knight had been somewhat obsessed, always hunting that... Lancelot's eyes widened.

"You don't mean—"

"I do. Glatisant is here. In the Midwest, at least. I've got the trail."

Which meant he was close to cashing in on a whole lot of points. Not that Lancelot was all that concerned. Even if Palomides banked big, Lancelot would catch up. It wasn't like the game was difficult for him. Just keep going east, and whenever you're in a place where someone needs help, you have to stop. If someone needs a lift, or their house painted, or a package delivered across the globe, you have to stop and take care of it before moving on or collecting any more points. The points were awarded depended on the difficulty and how fast you could circle the globe. Capturing Glatisant, the Questing Beast itself, would be worth a fortune. No one had managed it in over a hundred years. It, too, was ageless, and as long as they didn't kill it they could keep hunting it forever. It made things interesting. And dangerous. Just like Lancelot liked. He smiled.

"And you're telling me to gloat?" Lancelot asked.

"No, I'm asking if you want to help." That smile never widened. It remained small, amused. Lancelot wondered what the angle was. He felt a flutter of warmth in his chest, the stirring of his old urge to quest, to win. If Palomides was challenging him, he wouldn't back down, no matter where their adventures took them.

"You don't mind splitting the points with me?" Lancelot asked. It was the rules, after all, but Palomides spread his hands wide as if showing he was unarmed, or disinterested. Lancelot paused. It was possible there was some other game going on here, some angle that Palomides was working. But the bait was just too tempting.

"Maybe I just know more than most not to go up against Glatisant alone," Palomides said. "It has killed me a few times before."

Lancelot frowned. It was hardly amusing to think of death, even if it didn't end up meaning all that much to them. Dying put your points on hold, and it could take some time to grow old enough to play again. At the moment Lancelot was in his early thirties, Palomides a little younger, maybe twenty-five and looking far too good to die yet. Being reset now would be bad, much worse then going at sixty or even fifty, when there weren't many good years left for gaming anyway.

"Okay," Lancelot said. "I accept."

When Palomides said "a little north" he must have been being generous. Northern Wisconsin was hardly anywhere, just a large swath of trees and cold, even in October. They arrived at the hotel Palomides had picked out, and Lancelot shivered and watched Palomides slip out of the Jeep and stretch. They always looked more or less how they had the first time, that first life ages ago.

Lancelot got distracted watching Palomides, the way his shirt pulled up as he reached above his head, revealing a small patch of skin, the faint line of hair that led down into his pants.

"Where exactly are we?" he asked, and Palomides took a deep breath like he didn't mind the chill at all and looked around.

"Rhinelander," Palomides said. "Home of the *hodag*."

"The what?" Lancelot knew most monsters in the world, had hunted nearly all of them over the years, but had never heard of a hodag. It sounded like some sort of insult a child would make up

"The hodag. Something a professional liar came up with back in the day by gluing things to a badger. It's supposed to be something like a dragon, but with a frog's face and great big claws."

"Sounds like a few men I've known." Lancelot laughed.

"Glatisant looks something like that. And in the last few weeks the number of hodag sightings has skyrocketed around here. There's even some amateur video."

"So we're not the only ones looking for it?" If there were normal monster hunters out looking for it, there could be a problem. Part of the game was to not draw too much attention to themselves. They were to try and stay out of the spotlight, or too many questions might get asked.

"I'm saying that we need to be careful, yes."

Lancelot's frown deepened. Careful was not something he did well.

At the desk, Lancelot got them a room with a king-sized bed while Palomides unpacked a few things from the car.

When they arrived at the room, Palomides glanced at the bed without comment.

"It's all they had," Lancelot said with a playful smile, but Palomides just shrugged and produced his smart phone. He proceeded to show Lancelot where the sightings had been. They sat, leg to leg, as Palomides pointed out each one.

"So they're concentrated around this lake here?" Lancelot asked, tapping the screen. Palomides hummed his affirmative and brushed against Lancelot's finger as he had the map zoom out. Lancelot nudged closer against Palomides' leg, but when he looked over he saw Palomides looking at the map, ignoring him. Lancelot sighed.

"Bloom Lake. Right along the north shore, with most of them along Trails End Road." Palomides' voice was flat, downright clinical. Had Lancelot imagined the heat he had felt when their fingers had touched?

"I don't think I like the sound of that." Lancelot said. He had an aversion to endings. Kind of why he liked Hollywood movies, because nothing ever really ended. Just wait twenty years for the reboot. It made a familiar kind of sense to him.

"I'm afraid that's where we have to start." Palomides stood and slipped the phone back into his pocket.

"Do we have to go so soon?" Lancelot asked, falling back onto the bed. "We've only just arrived. After all that driving I think we've earned a soak in the hot tub and maybe a raid on the minibar."

He was beginning to get annoyed that Palomides seemed to have only the Questing Beast on his mind. For the entire trip so far he had seemed... not quite cold, really. But distant. Professional. Except that he would go out of his way to initiate touch, to brush against Lancelot's hand or shoulder or butt, to talk softly so that Lancelot had to lean close to hear. And all the while ignoring Lancelot's advances and feigning innocence. Lancelot just wanted to grab the man and toss him onto the bed.

"After," Palomides said, and Lancelot nearly growled. But he did get back to his feet, pushed his long hair behind his ears, and followed the taller man out to the car.

He took the passenger seat and Palomides got behind the wheel, reached for a pair of sunglasses hanging from the rearview. His hand missed, bumping them to the floor at Lancelot's feet. And before Lancelot could react, Palomides leaned completely over the armrest, hand retrieving the glasses while his face was less than a foot from Lancelot's lap.

"Oops," Palomides said, turning his head to smile up at Lancelot but not moving otherwise. Lancelot sucked in a breath, felt his body react to the sudden proximity, his cock throbbing slightly, flushing with heat. He wanted this, wanted Palomides to take him, wanted to take Palomides in turn, but then Palomides was back in his seat. Without another word Palomides started the car and pulled away, leaving Lancelot grasping for what to do with his frustration and budding erection.

They reached Trails End Road and Palomides got out first. They hadn't spoken the entire trip. Lancelot kept trying to think of something witty, something funny, but nothing seemed appropriate. He cursed at himself inwardly. He was Lancelot, Knight of the Round Table, and here he was acting like a shy maiden. His heart was racing, and he was fairly certain it wasn't because of the Questing Beast.

Together they affixed their sword belts and left the road. The woods were dense and blushing with fall colors. There was no avoiding the dead leaves, and they crunched as they walked, drawing farther and farther into the forest. Lancelot never really liked the autumn. Or rather, he hated winter, when the cold forced everyone inside, into their own personal cages, into layers of clothes that took ages to peel off. And autumn reminded him that winter was coming, which was almost as bad. He shivered.

Every few minutes they would stop and Palomides would check his phone, or retie his shoes, making sure to bend over as he did, his jeans showing the smooth curve of his ass.

"You ever have sex in the woods?" Lancelot asked. He was tired of being subtle, and his cock was hard, pushed up into the waistband of his pants to avoid being conspicuous. If he didn't fuck or kill something soon there was going to be trouble.

Palomides kept scanning the ground and trees. "A few times," he said. "If I recall correctly, it normally leads to getting dirty and sore."

"Not if you're good at it," Lancelot said, though that was something of a lie. The truth was he didn't care as long as the sex happened, and he was sure by the time they were done they wouldn't mind so much the dirt and leaves and sore muscles. There was, after all, a hot tub back at the hotel.

"And you're so sure you're that good?"

Lancelot laughed, light and arrogant, the way he had always laughed. Of course he was that good. He was Lancelot.

It was then that the forest erupted around him. With a crash, a tree was brushed to the side and Lancelot ducked and dove out of the way as a creature stormed past. Lancelot had never managed to track down the Questing Beast, had never even seen it before. Legend was that few could; only those, like Palomides, who had devoted themselves to tracking it. But Lancelot had it now, would prove that he was the greatest, would capture it on his very first try. It was bigger than Lancelot had expected, about the size of a small car and fast on those stubby legs. It screeched as it slammed into another tree and turned back.

"Move," Palomides called, and Lancelot's training and lifetimes of action brought him to his feet, drew the sword from his waist. He didn't run, didn't panic. He stood tall and ready, didn't even glance to see if Palomides was ready before charging at the creature.

His attack seemed to surprise it, and he managed to land a blow to its shoulder before it turned, tail whipping around. Lancelot threw himself back and out of the way as the tail impacted a tree trunk, pulverizing it. Palomides was in right away, swinging his own sword, scoring a hit on its side, nearing its neck. Screeching, the beast bounded away from them, into the trees.

Lancelot pursued, hand tightening around the hilt of his sword. No one escaped him once he made up his mind. The creature fled, but not fast enough, and Lancelot leapt, landed on its back, stabbed into the creature's shoulder. It lurched, and Lancelot slid forward, found himself falling, weightless until he hit the ground and rolled to a stop. The creature roared, and Lancelot crouched, realizing that he didn't have his sword.

Over the centuries Lancelot had gotten used to staring down Death. But as he saw Glatisant rear up, huge eyes fixed in hatred on him, Lancelot felt a sudden pang of regret that had nothing to do with failing to capture the monster. It was that he hadn't done more with the damned fool who had brought him this far. Palomides.

And like that, the man himself charged in, Palomides' sword flashing in the crisp air, drawing a wide red line across the creature's chest. Glatisant balked and rolled backward, and Lancelot spotted his sword, dove to retrieve it. A moment later he was on his feet and the Questing Beast was into the trees again, in full retreat.

Lancelot's heart was beating fast, his blood pounding in his veins. He raised his sword and pushed forward, hot to follow, to track the beast, to finally catch Glatisant. But before he could move three steps he realized that Palomides was standing still, watching him with that small smile he had been wearing in Chicago. It stopped him, made him pause in his pursuit.

"What is it?" Lancelot asked. Something about that smile bothered him, as if it was catching him in something embarrassing or wrong.

"It is true what they say about you, then," he said. "That it's the chase that gets you going."

"What?" Lancelot asked, incapable at that moment of forming a coherent reply. What *who* said about him? The chase? All he wanted to do was hunt down the monster that had attacked them and maybe then wash off the ick and fuck. But Palomides stood still, shaking his head slowly.

"Like with Guinevere," Palomides said, and Lancelot's hand tightened around the hilt of his sword. Most people knew better than to mention her. "All that talk of love eternal, all those stolen moments, and when you're finally free to be with her for eternity you run off to play this game instead. Where is she now? Living like a monk in Sweden?"

Lancelot considered turning around, walking away. Horny or not, he didn't have to stand there while Palomides analyzed and questioned his decisions. Guinevere had never been so serious a thing. Sure, he had enjoyed the jousts, the stolen kisses, the times they would fuck in Arthur's bed, but he had fucked Arthur on that bed just as many times. It wasn't about love, though that's what everyone else seemed to think. But he had come to terms with his past, with his first life, ages ago. He and Guinevere and Arthur had all made their peace and moved on. Why be bogged down by history? Lancelot wanted to be judged in the moment, in the now.

"I think it's the chase you're after. You weren't interested in Glatisant at all until he came charging through here, and now you're hot to follow. You're like a dog after a bone."

"What's it to you?" Lancelot asked, stepping forward. A part of him wanted to duel the man right there and be done. He was still Lancelot, still unbeaten. "What do you care what I do, who I love or don't love?"

Lancelot barely noticed Palomides move, but suddenly the man was in front of him, tall frame sweeping forward aggressively. Lancelot jumped back, sword rising from his side to hover between them. The small smile on Palomides' face was gone, replaced by something Lancelot could only describe as hungry.

"Maybe I wonder what it would take to keep your interest," Palomides said. "Maybe I wonder how to last more than a week in your bed. Maybe I've seen all the others topped by the great Lancelot and left to wander afterward alone and heartbroken and I don't want to end up that way."

Lancelot huffed. He really wasn't that bad. He never led anyone on. He let them know from the start that he was only in it for the sex, for the thrill. If some of them got more involved than he did, it was hardly his fault.

"Wait. You mean... you want...."

"You," Palomides said, finishing the thought, and he brushed Lancelot's sword aside as he stepped closer and let his own blade fall to the ground. Lancelot started to back away but Palomides was already to him, hands wrapping around the back of his neck, tangling his long hair, pulling him into a fierce kiss.

"Wait," Lancelot said, breaking the kiss, struggling with the rush of new circumstances. Wasn't he still angry about the Guinivere thing? But Palomides' tongue exploring his mouth was distracting, and it felt so good to have the taller man's body pressed against his, their cocks, erect and straining against their jeans, rubbing each other through the denim. He dropped his sword as well.

"If I wait you'll just lose interest," Palomides said, and Lancelot didn't think that was fair but he didn't argue as Palomides' hands dropped to the buttons of his pants. Some things were better to just accept, and Lancelot was confident he could handle anything that happened.

At least, he was confident of it until Palomides reached a warm hand into his pants, sliding down the naked length of his erection. Closing his eyes, Lancelot concentrated on not going off too soon, despite how excited he was. Despite how he wanted to get back at Palomides for having made him wait for so long.

Together they moved so that Lancelot's back was against a tree, and Palomides took the opportunity to use his free hand to undo Lancelot's sword belt and tug down his jeans and boxers, revealing his cock to the open air. Lancelot gasped at the chill on his thighs, but Palomides was doing more than enough to make sure he didn't get cold.

"Seems like someone's a bit eager," Palomides said, breaking the kiss, trailing soft nips down Lancelot's neck.

"Like you didn't know what you were d—" Lancelot could barely stifle a moan as Palomides gave his cock a gentle squeeze and then knelt before him. Strong hands quested up and down his legs, and Lancelot whimpered slightly as he felt Palomides' hot breath on his smaller head. The air was crisp, with a faint smell of wet earth and blood from their fight with the Questing Beast. Had that been only a moment ago? Strange how things seemed to blend together now, and Lancelot felt his body buck forward as Palomides' mouth engulfed his cock.

Lancelot leaned back against the tree, hands finding Palomides' short hair. He wanted to push forward, to thrust, but Palomides held his hips, refused to let him. Slowly he took Lancelot in an inch, two, then stopped. Lancelot felt his cock throb with frustration as Palomides backed off, then took him again only that far.

"You could at least do a proper job," Lancelot said though gritted teeth. Palomides just smiled and stood, hands going to his own sword belt and pants, which he quickly had open and pushed down. His cock bounced free, and Lancelot swallowed.

"Care to show me how?" Palomides asked. Lancelot growled and kicked his pants completely off, pulled his shirt up and over his head at the same time so he was completely naked. He stood, glowering, wondering less how he had gotten into this situation and more how he was going to make the man in front of him pay for teasing him.

He started by grabbing the bottom of Palomides' shirt and slipping his hands inside, letting them glide over hard muscles. He found that small trail of hair and followed it up with his mouth, found Palomides' navel and dipped his tongue in, heard a gasp and felt him squirm beneath the touch. The air was still cold and the forest around them was silent, waiting breathless for him to continue. He did, pulling off Palomides' shirt as his mouth traced muscles up until he found a nipple. Lancelot played his tongue along the skin where nipple met chest and felt Palomides squirm again.

"Not so talkative now," Lancelot said, and gave the nipple a soft nip.

Hands appeared on his shoulders, pushing him down, and Lancelot didn't fight it, let himself drop until he was eye level with Palomides' cock. For a moment he only looked, admired the gentle curve upward, the flushed head that seemed to pulse gently. Lancelot licked his lips and then opened his mouth.

Palomides moaned as Lancelot took him as deep as he could, going slow so he didn't gag. When he couldn't go any further he paused, getting used to the girth, then pulled out, sucking gently as he went. He pushed back down, increasing the pace, using one hand to cup Palomides' sack and the other to grasp the base of his cock, steadying it as he pushed down again and again.

"I think I see your point," Palomides said, voice strained. "Your technique is definitely better." Lancelot liked the sound of that, the barely controlled pleasure leaking into Palomides' words. He was Lancelot, after all. Instead of answering, though, he just went even faster, concentrating on not pushing too deep, on not gagging, but determined to push Palomides' cock right to the brink.

Before he could press faster, though, Palomides stepped back and his cock pulled free of Lancelot's mouth with an audible pop. Lancelot himself tried to follow forward but found a hand on his shoulder, stopping him. He looked up, annoyed, only to find that familiar, infuriating smile waiting for him.

"Have something in mind?" Lancelot asked, wondering if Palomides would ever let either of them get off. The taller man laughed and pulled Lancelot up. And then in one motion he backed Lancelot back up against the tree again and stood with his legs slightly bent, his own feet on either side of Lancelot's so that he was nearly straddling him. Their bodies pressed together, their cocks touching.

"I thought we might have something of a joust," Palomides said, and Lancelot hissed in a breath as Palomides' large hand wrapped around both their cocks.

"What does the winner get?" Lancelot managed to ask. Laughter was his answer. Palomides held up his free hand and spit into it, presented it to Lancelot to do the same. Without lube it would have to do. Lancelot spit and then took a ragged breath as Palomides took his slick hand and started pumping over both their cocks at once, the undersides rubbing together. Lancelot shuddered and leaned back into the tree, wrapped his arms around Palomides' firm ass to keep him from falling back.

"You think you'll get bored of this?" Palomides asked, and Lancelot grunted, didn't want to answer, didn't want to think of anything but the pleasure he was feeling, the tingle that was working its way from his balls and into his stomach. If Palomides stopped now he would kill him.

"I'm...." Lancelot started to warn but Palomides just pumped faster and Lancelot let himself go, let the feeling spread from his stomach to his limbs and finally back into his cock, where it released in a hot stream up and over Lancelot's chest, over his stomach, over Palomides' stomach and both of their cocks. Lancelot gasped and squirmed as Palomides kept moving, kept pumping despite the intense sensations. Lancelot endured, felt the pace falter, and opened his eyes to see Palomides gasp and climax, his eyes closing, his mouth opening as he came. Lancelot watched as the same face that had smirked in frustrating confidence melted away into shuddering pleasure, teeth gritting to let in staccato breaths as Lancelot felt new jets of warmth spatter his body. It was a face

Lancelot had never seen before on Palomides, and one that he felt the strong urge to know better, to see again and again and again.

Finally Palomides slowed to a stop and they both heaved in great breaths, their bodies shivering in the sudden cold, the sudden absence of their pleasure. Lancelot gave a small chuckle.

"I guess you won," he said, knowing that he had fallen first. So much for Lancelot the unbeaten. Not that he minded. "What were the stakes again?"

"Well," Palomides said, making a show of thinking hard. "I did say I didn't want to end up like all the others who had been topped by the great Lancelot. So maybe—"

"Not without lube," Lancelot said hastily. Other thoughts threatened to crowd into his mind. Weren't they in the woods for a reason? Probably not worth thinking about. Palomides' smile left no room for other thoughts, anyway.

"Then I'm sure we can work something out."

And they did, with their hands and their mouths, on the forest floor and in high branches of the trees. And Lancelot discovered that with Palomides' tongue priming him, the lube wasn't required after all.

Lancelot woke some time later. His whole body was shivering, and absently he reached out for Palomides, to pull him closer. Only Palomides wasn't there. Eyes opened quickly, found the woods around him empty, silent. He sat up.

There was no sign of where Palomides had gone. Or where Lancelot's clothes had gone. Had he thrown them up a tree? It was possible, but he didn't think so. Damn it was cold. He moved to stand and that's when he saw the note, a small folded piece of paper that obviously didn't belong. Lancelot hoped it was just Palomides letting him know he had gone back to the car to get more stuff.

Lancelot picked up the note and quickly read it. *I'm pretty sure*

Glatisant will be moving on after this. I'm betting north, into Canada. I think I'll follow it. Maybe I'll see you around. PS. I took the car. Good luck. He read the words three times to make sure he got it right. Then he crumpled the paper and threw it onto the ground.

That bastard. That sneaking, conniving bastard. He would pay for this. There was no way Lancelot was going to let him get away with it, get away with making a fool out of him. Oh, let him run, but Lancelot would track him down. It would be his quest, and when he caught up he'd make sure to even the score. And then some. He'd leave the man handcuffed to a buoy in Hudson Bay. Or at least to a hotel bed in the Hudson Bay Hotel. A small smile crept over Lancelot's face.

Maybe everything that Palomides had said was true. Maybe all he did care about was the chase. They'd just have to see. But Lancelot did know one thing: it was going to be fun finding out.

And, steeling himself against the cold, Lancelot picked a direction and started walking, hot on his latest quest.

The Giving Game
Alexandra Erin

It was the seventh day of Christ's Mass before last, the eve of the new year, when the knight dressed in greenery rode into Camelot's great hall. He seemed a brute, yet I found him a remarkable figure: unclad but for the vines and leaves entwining his limbs, revealing more than they concealed and suggesting more still.

His limbs were supple and corded, strong and flexible as green wood. While his lined, learned face spoke of endless ages of experience, there was youth in his form. Youth, and power, and perhaps something more.

He dismounted his steed as lightly as taking a step. He strode purposefully, his bare feet making barely a sound on the flagstones of the hall.

We all stood transfixed by the incongruity of it all. Someone asked what Yuletide amusement had Sir Kay dreamed up this time. I would have laughed—in disbelief rather than mirth—if I could but have forced any sound from my throat.

This was no holiday mummery. He was of nature, but there was something more than natural about him, something beyond the mundane. Something wonderful.

No one reached for a sword, even when he slung the axe off his back. His fluid, easy motions carried no threat. The genial smile that lit that ageless, aged face he wore so well disarmed us.

The bejeweled axe gleamed like no other, more treasure than tool. Yet I fancied I could see the sharpness from where I stood.

His challenge rang out: A holiday game, he called it, to pass the time. He would offer that beautiful crescent axe to whichever knight would wield it against him for the space of one blow, but only if the same knight were willing to accept a blow from him in return a year and a day later.

No one accepted.

No one dared.

I heard you stirring, and the spell broke for me.

I know what is said: that Gawain moved to protect the king from whatever hidden danger this bewitching man and his strange game held. Such faith is humbling, but I am not so certain that I did not stumble forward because it brought me closer to the verdant figure. I am not so certain that I did not move because I longed to hold his beautiful weapon in my own hands. I am not so certain that I had any thought in my head at all more than want, than *need*.

I am certain of nothing, save that I stepped forward and barked what unworthy reply I could muster.

He saluted my incoherence most charitably. On leaden legs, I lumbered toward him. With spritely stride, he stepped toward me. In the middle, we met as men. He clapped me on the back and drew me close in a one-armed embrace. His touch was surprisingly soft and surpassingly warm.

On him, I smelled the forest: wet, loamy earth and mossy trees. I smelled all the flowers of spring, asleep under the snow. I smelled the beasts of the field, stirring in their dens as the old year died and the new one was born.

Behind and beneath it all, I smelled the rich musk of man, and I knew that this was no apparition. Here stood a man, subject to all the rigors and exertions of manhood. He sweat like me. That was evident. Perhaps he would bleed like me.

Perhaps he could die.

In that moment, fear undid me. I did not fear for my own life, but what I might do in defense of it. If I withheld my best violence, would he not still do his worst against me? Yet if I struck true, might I not bring the end of something wonderful?

I have always displayed a proper reverence for the supernatural, and yet I have never been a man of superstition. In that moment I was almost overwhelmed with dread at the thought that in striking down this green knight I would doom us all.

What if the newborn year were strangled in its crib? What if the sun never returned, if the thaw never came? What if the fields never sprouted and fruits died on the vine?

"Come, lad," the knight said, holding out the axe. "Do you fear what I may do to you?"

"No, good sir," I replied, my mouth full of dry porridge. "I do not."

"Then do not insult me to think that I fear anything you might do to me," he said.

The reproach was gentle, but genuine. Shamed, I took the axe.

We have called it an axe, but truly it is only the size and heft that made it so. Its curve was closer to being a sickle, and the make of it bore some resemblance to the ceremonial blades the ancient brothers of the grove use to harvest mistletoe and blood. Yet this was no farmer's tool, nor any mere ritual ornament. It could serve as a weapon of war.

The knight in green knelt, offering his head.

"Strike," he bade me. "Let nothing stay your hand, if it be not the fear of what comes in return."

It was not honor or vanity that moved me to swing as I did, but the desire that I might please this strange visitor with my obedience.

Heaven help me, I swung the sickle-axe.

I can see the scene unfold behind my eyes. Sometimes it comes to me at night, unbidden. This happens less and less in the days since my quest has been completed.

One strike separated his beautiful head from his shoulders. The blow was blessedly bloodless. His body shuddered and then fell, twitching weakly on the flagstones. His head bounced twice and then rolled to a stop, eyes staring unfocused at the ceiling.

His lips twitched. It seemed to me that he gasped as his body spent its last spasm, but there was no sound.

A great cheer went up from all around the hall. If I said that it touched me not, I would not speak the half of it. It touched me as an ice wind touches skin through a shirt of mail. It ran through me like a spit does a boar. It left me gutted and hollow, and hung up to dry.

I feared the knight's game had been a prophecy, for I could not imagine a future that stretched beyond a year and a day.

I could see that I might live with the enormity of this crime for a while, that I might make some poor attempts to atone for what I had done, but then winter would come again, and all the festive revelry would serve no purpose other than to remind me of what I had done. Then would come the eve of the new year after, the anniversary of my crime, and perhaps then it would become too much, that I should live while he was dead... and then the blow I'd dealt would fall upon me.

This strange fancy passed through my head before the cheering had died away.

That is where this tale moved from the uncanny to the fantastic.

For no sooner had the hurrahs ceased than the light came back to the knight's eyes and he laughed. He laughed! There was no wind in his lungs, I am sure, and even if there was, what had they to do with his mouth anymore? Yet he laughed, and I laughed with him.

How brave I must have seemed, to be struck with mirth at the sight of this lithe giant of a man pushing himself up off the floor while his head lay several feet apart from his neck. How bold, to have offered him my hand. How gallant I must have looked, picking up his head—his own head, even!—and offering it to him after gently kissing the crown where he had been bruised on the flagstones.

By his miraculous resurrection, I was condemned, and yet I cared not. What could that be, if not courage?

I did not feel courageous or mirthful. Principally, what I felt was hysterical relief. I stood not condemned, but reprieved. He lived!

While I stood thunderstruck, the knight—head under his shoulder—mounted his great steed with easy grace. His parting call was for me to meet him in the green chapel on the appointed day.

The outward flourishes of these events were known to you already. The rest I have told so that you might better understand what follows from this point.

The year passed in its good own time, as years are wont to do. For no man does the wheel of time stop, nor for anything will it be entreated to speed its passage.

Never did I dread what was coming, only the possibility of failure. I feared to disappoint my green knight. Dying at his hand would be nothing compared to dying without seeing him again.

Always, I was acutely aware of my approaching appointment. I had no knowledge of anything that might be termed a green chapel, and only one thought as to who might know.

The founding of Camelot and the spirit of unity brought with it had brought the druids back out of the shadows to enjoy a rare period of peace with us, their Christian brethren. It was to them I went first.

Sadly, while the learned brotherhood's answer was no doubt steeped in knowledge, "all the world is one great temple, all green places chapels within it, and the Green Man may be found in them all" did not answer my needs. We as Christians are told that wheresoever we may gather in praise is a church, but if this makes the whole world one great cathedral, it does not make it easier to locate an individual petitioner within it.

God was certainly omnipresent, and the druids' Green Man may in his own small way have been as well, but my knight in green had told me to come for him at the green chapel, which suggested a place in particular.

Many times did I ride out into the wood and countryside to seek this place or any word or sign of my knight. Always was I disappointed. There were many false trails and no true ones. The thought of seeing my green knight sustained me during my long nights on the road. It kept me in the saddle during my days and awake during my nights.

At the equinox, I rode out for what I knew would be my final quest. If I failed to find the chapel in the allotted time, I would take my own life in as near a fashion to the blow owed me as my own hand could muster. It would be said I died for honor.

At last, I headed north to the woods of Caledon, where our

own Merlin dwelt in the wild for so long. What other wondrous things might grow there in the deep wood?

Many of the sights I encountered along the way would make for their own tales if told in full, but I must now pass over them to speak of what transpired just after midwinter, when I came upon the castle in the woods.

It was a marvelous place, and marvelously out of place, miles from any other habitation. In shape, it was a dwelling such as any of your chief vassals might claim, yet its construction was quite singular. The walls were of unworked stone and hard-packed earth that seemed to have grown between great trees, many of which still held broad-bladed leaves in the depths of December.

I could see that a hunter dwelled within, for the device upon the flags was a pair of horns, and many fine trophies hung over the arched entryway. I had the curious fancy as I looked upon it that I had found the hunting lodge of some great lord of the other realm, some faerie king.

Though the lands around were desolate of people, the place was inhabited. I could hear the sounds of music and revelry. The windows in the high towers were lit. The smell of roasting meat carried out into the cold night air.

Christian or pagan, I could not say, but the folk within would not be found faithless, I was certain, for they made the accustomed revelry for the season. Could there have been a better time for a stranger to walk into a castle uninvited and unannounced? After all, this was much how the adventure had begun. There would be such a pleasing symmetry, should it end thusly.

I had no real reason to hope that this strange castle would furnish me with an end to my quest. There was something of the green about the place, but fantastic as it was, it was no chapel. Yet does one need a reason for hope? Does hope require or even give recourse to reason?

Let me find my knight within, I prayed. *Let these halls be his.*

There was time before the reckoning. If I could spend it in his company before the blow fell, it would all be worth it.

I bid a passing page tell me where I had found myself. He seemed a canny lad, in both senses of the word. There was nothing of verdant magic or another world about him, yet he was sharp as a nail. He let me know that I had found the castle of Lord Bertilak, a lord unknown in the south, and Lady Bertilak, his wife.

I attempted to frame some question about the lord's general appearance and habits that would allow me to ascertain whether this Bertilak and my knight in green were one and the same without offering offense, but my wits were too slow, and the lad was off.

Knowing the answer beforehand would have done no more than steeled me for despair. One look at Lord Bertilak revealed that he was fully mortal, and not my knight all in green.

There was power in his limbs, yes. There was grace in his bearing. There was comeliness in the lined face beneath his graying curls. At first blush, I took these things in not at all, so bitter was my disappointment.

But I had not shied from asking the meanest beggar or the smallest child I met on the road if they had any knowledge of the green knight or his green chapel. Here was this great lord in this improbable forest fastness. Would I not stoop to ask him?

Girded by my position as a knight of Camelot, I made bold to approach him at his table. He sat with his handsome wife on his right side, both at the head of the long board where his favored vassals dined. Many of them eyed me as I approached, but it was a time of feasting and my hands were empty and wide in greeting.

"Hail, Lord Bertilak," I said. "Hail, Lady Bertilak. Hail, good knights of this fine castle. Sir Gawain gives you good greetings of Arthur, High King of all Britons."

"King of Cornwall, he means," I think I heard someone mutter with a snort, but it was the holidays, and in this land beyond our ken it seemed a poor place to correct the matter.

"We are well greeted," Lady Bertilak said, raising a wooden goblet and gracing me with a smile. The wine had left her lips glistening and red. I had taken her in even less than her husband, which was a mistake, for she cut a regal figure. She was mature, as her husband was. They seemed a couple well matched.

"I think we are not," her lord said, though there was a merry twinkle in his dark eyes. "He would have better greeted you first, my love. Are we not equals in fact?"

"Be still, good husband of my heart," the lady did reply. "Would you have him speak our titles at the same time, each out of one corner of his mouth? He did greet you first this time. He may greet me first the next, and amend the balance. Does that satisfy?"

"It may, in time," he said. He got to his feet and thrust out an arm, which I gratefully clasped. "We have heard of your king, and we approve of his great designs. The hospitality of our castle is yours. Join the feast!"

"Thank you, my Lady Bertilak, my Lord Bertilak," I said. "I shall find a bench with room to hold me."

"Nonsense!" Lady Bertilak said. "You are our most honored guest, good sir, and you sit at our table."

I did not have to glance down the rows again to know for certain that the high table was packed elbow to elbow. Any place I took would belong to another with a prior claim. Knight of the Round Table or not, I was a stranger in a strange land.

"My lady," I demurred, "I would not dream of displacing any one of your worthy vassals. I am arrived late to the feast through no fault but my own folly. I beg you, let me find my own place, wherever it may be."

"What, man? Would you sit with the dogs by the fire?" Lord Bertilak asked.

My humility has often been noted at court. I do make some small admission here that I know well what a becoming effect it may have on some persons, so it was with hope that we might find an amicable compromise that I looked the lord of the strange castle square in the eye and said, "If you think they would have me."

He laughed. They all laughed. I felt a surge of excitement that I could only think of then as triumph.

"Tell me," the lady said. "Is it true that in the great court of the High King, the table is round so that none may sit at the head?"

"It is true," I said.

"Then you must today sit with us, at the head of ours," she said. "It will be quite the novelty for us all."

I could have kissed her. By treating me as a curiosity and the whole thing as a jest, she shielded me from the enmity of her retainers, and yet allowed me to preserve some dignity.

The stool the servants brought forth and placed between the great carved chairs of Lady and Lord Bertilak was quite a bit ruder than either of those seats, but so often had I sat upon the ground or a stump or even taken my meals in the saddle that it seemed to be a throne.

Of course, the quality of the furniture had no bearing on the quality of the feast, nor the company, both of which were excellent.

The Lord and Lady Bertilak were a delight, separately and together. He was, as I had surmised, something of a hunter. She was a poet, and quite the wit. They did indeed rule their lands together. Queens in their own right have a long precedent among the Celts, and the woman who was now Lady Bertilak had been the one to propose joining her lands to those of her now-husband through the union of marriage. They had both divested themselves of their original names, taking their present ones from the castle.

"What was your name before?" I asked her.

"What was yours, before you were born?" she asked, and with this mirthful reproach, she did give me cause to know that I had strayed too far out of bounds.

"My lady, I apologize," I said, and asked nothing more of their history, though I longed to know how the wondrous castle had come to be, and how it had come to be theirs.

"Sir Gawain, do you hunt?" Lord Bertilak asked me, a bit later on.

"I have hunted all this year, yet ever my quarry eludes me," I said.

"Perhaps you have been looking in the wrong place, good Gawain," Lady Bertilak said.

"Aye, indeed," her husband said. "The hunting ground is of paramount importance, lad. Once you've found the right place, the search is half over."

"I think it would be all over," I said. "It is a place that I hunt."

I told them of my quest. I did not then reveal to them all that I have told you now in confidence, but only the barest of the facts: the entry of the knight into the hall, his challenge, my acceptance, and his retort.

"You must be quite brave," Lady Bertilak said when my short tale was concluded.

"My bravery is not the matter," I said. "I have less than a week in which to fulfill my promise, and no idea where to look."

"No further!" Lord Bertilak said. "The green chapel is known to us. It lies less than two miles hence, along a well-worn path."

"You speak truly?"

"I do," he said.

"He does," his wife agreed.

"Then I have prevailed upon your hospitality long enough—"

Two sets of hands grabbed my own as I made to rise.

"Stay," Lady Bertilak said.

"Please," Lord Bertilak added. "Would you pass your days in the snow, with naught but pine boughs for your roof? The appointed hour is not upon you. Pass the holidays with us, in warmth and humor. During the days you can ride and hunt with me, and in the evening we shall feast! On the first day of the new year, I will deliver you."

"If this is amenable to you both, I can render no objection," I said.

Knowing the strange form of my hosts' dwelling, I did in the back of my mind have the memory of certain faerie stories, and so I was wary of some trick that would cause me to break my word or miss my appointment with the knight all in green. But refusing such a generous offer without better cause would have caused bad blood, whatever my hosts' nature might be.

The next day, my horse was saddled for me and I was given a spear and bow.

"Forgive an impish disposition," my male host said, "but your story last night did put me in mind of a similar holiday game we might play."

"My good lord, I fear I've had my fill of such games."

"I think you will like mine better, for it is not in the spirit of violence but generosity," he said. "You and I will have a hunting contest, but whatever good things I might take in the course of the day I will yield up to you, and whatever comes your way, you will give over to me. We will do the same tomorrow, and the next day, and the one after, and then see who does best in giving by the end of your stay. What say you, Gawain?"

I laughed. It seemed a novel contest, in truth.

"It seems a good way for a braggart to appear humble," I said.

"Then it should brook no objections from you," he said, and I knew that he had me.

"Very well," I said, and we rode out.

I am a passing hunter when it comes to feeding myself on the trail, but Lord Bertilak knew the land. Moreover, I was distracted both by the imminent end of my quest—and possibly my life beside—and by the prospect of yielding whatever I caught to him.

Understand, it was not meanness of spirit that stayed my hand. Quite the opposite. When I had a scrawny rabbit sighted down the shaft of my arrow, I stopped, imagining what it would be like to offer this poor tribute to a true hunter.

When we rode back to the castle, I had caught nothing but a slight chill, while Lord Bertilak had presented me with a brace of coneys, the least of which would have put my meager attempt to shame.

"My Lord Bertilak, I've lost my taste for the hunt," I said when it was time to ride out the next morning. "Pray forgive me, and release me from our contest."

"It's a poor knight who quits when he's behind," he said.

"Crown me the loser," I said. "I will hunt no more."

"Well, you are my guest and you must do as you like," he said.

"But our contest holds! I will give you what I catch, but you must give me whatever you gain while I am out on the hunt."

"You must not expect too much of me, my lord."

"I expect nothing more than you're given, my humble braggart."

And with that, he rode out to the hunt, and I retired to my room, where I immediately regretted having passed on a day's distraction, with the appointed time so near and the appointed place so close.

I did not have long to regret my decision, for my solitude did not last. There was a knock on the frame of my door, which had been left slightly ajar. The lady of the castle stood without.

"Please, enter!" I said quickly, rising to my feet. I was immediately aware that, having taken off my winter riding garb, I had not properly dressed again. The damage was done, though, for the lady was in the room. There I stood in tunic and hose, with not even drawers between. I was very conscious of the length of my tunic, or rather, the shortness of it.

"Good morning, good knight," she said. "Did the prospect of hunting with my husband not please you?"

Mindful of any insult-trap, I gave answer: "Say instead, my lady, that it pleased me to remain with you."

"I see how I please you," she said, her eyes darting downward for the space of a moment. "But a fair answer calls for a fair reward."

"The truth asks no reward for being pleasant."

"Would you refuse a kiss?" she said, laughing.

My breath caught in my throat.

This might sound peculiar, though perhaps it will not. It seems to me that the ways in which we men speak of love are quite limited in comparison to the ways that we feel it. I know this to be true of myself, and I do not imagine I am so exceptional in regard....

But I have no words to describe what I felt or why, and yet, I am charged to tell you the whole truth of what happened. Even if

I were not, I think—I feel—that I must attempt to express this, or it will drive me to distraction for the rest of my days.

My cock, to speak of it plainly, had begun to stir from the moment I was aware that it hung beneath the hem of my tunic. It surged to life at the sound of her laughter.

It was not the beauty of Lady Bertilak alone that I found exciting. It was something in our positions. I was unarmored and only partially clad, hardly the figure of a knight. She was in her fine gown, every inch the lady, with laughter ringing from her lips and dancing behind her eyes.

I had been in a state of greater undress in the presence of a woman before, and with a clear aim in mind. Yet never had the ardor coursed its path through my body faster or harder or straighter than when I stood there before that great lady, accidentally revealed.

"Your body gives answer, good Gawain," she teased, "but I must have an answer from your lips before you have a kiss from mine."

I closed my eyes.

"My lady," I breathed.

"Yes?"

"*Please.*"

My eyes remained closed. She might have left me standing there waiting and willing, penis rigid at attention and body shaking, and I would not have known until she was long gone. It would have been a fine joke, I supposed, and no more than I deserved.

The thought of that excited me more.

But then her lips were on mine, and the kiss was long, and hard, and deep in a way that surpasses my ability to describe it. I am a young knight. I have chased kisses, chaste kisses from fair maidens as well as those I hoped would prove a prelude to some further diversions, with mixed success.

I had never thought of a kiss as an intimacy all its own.

As a child, it was an imitation of affection. As an adult, it had become a stop along the way. The first kiss I shared with Lady Bertilak was an act unto itself, and yet I wanted more. I wanted to run my hands along her body. I wanted to tear her gown from her, if only as a way of wordlessly entreating her to so rend my tunic similarly. I wanted to push her so that she might push me back, might throw me to the floor and throw her leg over me as easily as her husband had mounted his stallion that morning.... I could not imagine mounting her, even if it had been my proper place to do so. I could scarcely credit the image of any man doing so, in that moment.

Yet the image of Lady Bertilak mounting me, seating herself upon the rigid shaft of my cock, riding it up and down at a pace of her choosing, wrenching all the sweet pleasure she desired from my body—this idea would not be denied. I was convinced that had she any desire of this, she would have taken it. In that realization, I felt some measure of rejection. She could see how she made me feel, I knew. She had to know that I would refuse her nothing, that my body was hers to dispose of as she saw fit. Yet, she saw fit to dispose with it entirely.

I have heard older men speak of this kind of treatment in the most debasing terms: ball-chopping, ball-shriveling, cock-withering. Strangely, though, this dejection did nothing to dampen the fire she had kindled within my loins. It surged hotter, burned brighter. I felt if she had paid a moment's attention to my cock, I would have embarrassed myself, if it were possible to be further embarrassed, by shuddering to an immediate climax. I also felt like I wouldn't have minded the embarrassment, if it didn't mean she left disappointed.

I suppose that I could have been bolder myself, if I had truly wanted more. Knowing little of the customs shared by lady-wife and lord-husband, it seemed too forward to assume that I could take advantage of everything Lady Bertilak might offer me without suffering consequences under the roof she shared with Lord Bertilak.

That, and she had only offered a kiss.

And then it was done, and I was alone again.

Many thoughts swirled and sparred in my head that day, but I could not begin to reconstruct and make sense of them.

Did I say could not? In fact, I dared not. The memory of her face so close before me would swim before my eyes, and no sooner could I chase it away then I would feel her lips pressed again against mine. I imagined those same lips, moving with the same bold confidence down to my chin, along the line of my jaw, down my neck, towards my chest. My pulse quickened as I imagined her progress down my body toward my stiffening cock, the one part of the fantasy that was no mere figment.

To banish that phantom sensation, I would focus my mind on the kiss as it had happened: two sets of lips pressed together, nothing more remarkable than that. Only then I would imagine that her hand had found the swelling knob of my cock, that it strained not against its confinement but against the squeezing of her fingers, her grip as firm as her manner had been.

Such sweet frustration! Such agonizing pleasure! I had gone much longer without relief, and thought myself quite pious for it. How easy it is to seem a saint when one has never known true temptation.

Twice during the day I ventured out into the halls only to find myself beating a retreat because an inconveniently lascivious reverie left my trousers sporting a horn that no amount of modest posture could conceal.

By day's end, I had confined myself to my room like a hermit, but I knew my seclusion could not last. In due time, Lord Bertilak returned and I was summoned to the great hall to receive his gift of the day, a fine stag he had shot that afternoon.

He presented it to me in front of all of his vassals and servants, during the early revels of the afternoon. Of course I directed that it be taken to the kitchen and prepared for the enjoyment of all, as I had no use for a whole hart. The gift was symbolic, though Lord Bertilak did direct that the antlers be saved along with the pelt for my use.

"And what have you for me?" he asked, with an impish air.

"My lord, I have passed the day in my room," I said. "I could give you the solitude I found there, but it was not restful and you would not thank me."

"You gained nothing?"

"No, my lord."

"Caught nothing?"

"No, my lord."

"Were given nothing, by no one?

"N... in fact, my lord," I said, pausing to gather my wits. Was this the faerie-trap I had feared? "I was given one thing."

"By rights of our contest, this belongs to me," he said. He held out a hand. "Wait no longer, sir, but give it over, so we might judge who is greatest in gifts."

"If my lord is sure he wants it, then perhaps it would be best if we could repair to some private chamber," I said, heat rising in my cheeks.

"I gave my gift in front of all, so you must do the same," he said. "Then we may all be judged fairly."

If this were indeed a faerie plot, then he knew well what was coming next. If not, then this might be accepted in good cheer and taken as a part of the holiday revels. So I told myself, to steel myself for what must follow.

I went to him, to give to him the same kiss I had been given by his wife, intending to match her motions as well as I could remember them. That was very well indeed. As scarcely as I could have dissected the events in my bedroom of the morning as they happened, I had been gifted with many long hours for my mind to stage it like a play until the sequence of it was seared into my brain and stitched into my heart.

My eyes had been shut against her approach, but I kept Lady Bertilak in my head as I advanced toward her husband. Doing so not only gave me a model to follow, but allowed me to see myself in some ways as simply a proxy between the two of them. I was merely giving to the husband what had been given to me by the wife. If one thought of it in those terms, then there could be no sin, for what was more natural than a wife bestowing upon her lord husband the affection he was due?

This might seem a hollow rationalization to salve my sin, but it was more than that. In faith, it made the whole thing more exciting for me. I tried to become the Lady Bertilak.

It started with a head tilt, a very slight tilt. A steely look in my eyes. The stride must be deliberate, not hurried but without a trace of trepidation. Reaching him, I reached behind his head, gathering in my fist a bunch of his curly hair and then pulling his head toward mine as much as I leaned in. My lips parted only slightly before contact. Stunned by my brash act, Lord Bertilak's mouth opened enough to admit my tongue.

I have heard it said that Bretons kiss in this fashion, though those who say so show no aversion to doing it themselves.

A kiss is not simply motions, though. It cannot be drilled by rote. To honor our wager, it was necessary that I give to my lord host all the passion and intensity my lady host had bequeathed unto me. I could not give a feeling that I did not feel in my heart, so at first it seemed like I must fail.

But when our lips touched, when the scruff on his chin touched my skin and I smelled the earthy tang of his sweat, I found the passion flowering within my soul. I remembered well how my spirit had stirred at the sight of my knight in green, and how often I had despaired of ever seeing him again before Lord Bertilak had revealed that the end of my quest was at hand. In that moment, he had given me a greater gift than a great stag or a deep kiss, deeply felt. I had desired his wife, but I loved him, and I let this love flow through me until I was not imitating the Lady Bertilak but kissing Lord Bertilak.

I was myself, Gawain, kissing this man who had become my salvation, and I meant it with all my heart and more.

As I made that shift, something in him seemed to shift. His tongue found mine. His lips moved not just in response to mine but in concert with them. His strong, rough hands were on my back. With a surge of gratitude I could not explain, I ceded control to him, and he bent me backward into a deep dip to finish our embrace.

When we broke apart, I sank down on knees of water, gasping raggedly for air. I noticed with an odd flush of pride that I had also bestowed upon him the same predicament his wife had left me in.

To say it plainly, he was as hard as the oak board of his table. So was I.

I don't think the laughter of the men and ladies of his court had much to do with the stiffening of his cock, but it only strengthened mine. It's true, I've always enjoyed playing the soul of humility, but I felt like I was discovering a deeper taste for it, though I knew not what to make of it.

After that interlude the night passed much the same as the preceding one. I sat at the head of the table, between my co-equal hosts. We enjoyed roasted venison and many other delights, along with music and dancing and juggling and other such pageantry as the holidays bring.

I could not help stealing glances to judge the results of my handiwork—or lipwork, if you will—between the legs of my Lord Bertilak. No doubt a simple response of the physiology to stimulus, as Merlin might have said, but I found myself wondering if he might not be affected as deeply by my affection as I had been by his wife's. Would he spend the next day wound to distraction by sensual visitations at odd moments? Would the memory of my lips stay on his? Would he imagine them wandering downward? Would his cock grow by throbbing degrees as my lips got closer to it, in the theater of his mind?

To think of him imagining my lips on his body put me to imagining his body beneath my lips. It was a queer thought, to be sure, but I had found myself in a queer place.

The next day, there was no conversation before Lord Bertilak rode out.

I do not know if I hoped that Lady Bertilak would call upon me again, but as I had not dressed for riding out, I was dressed when she did.

"My lady, I think this game has gone far enough," I said.

"The only game is between my husband and yourself," she said. "What is between you and me is up to you and me."

"Is that your custom, here in Castle Bertilak?" I asked.

"We make our own customs," she said.

"I have no wish to dishonor myself," I said. "Nor bring dishonor to you."

"Could your hands be sullied by touching something clean?" she asked.

"No, my lady."

"Then you cannot dishonor yourself with me, nor could I with you," she said. "To prove it, I will touch you... if you wish."

I thought about what it would mean, when her husband returned. Oddly, this did not help me to make up my mind one way or the other.

But I nodded.

"I will have it from your lips, good Gawain," she said.

"Aye, my Lady Bertilak," I said. "I do wish."

This time I kept my eyes open as she kissed me, as her hand fished beneath my clothes for my already-hard cock. She found it, and went to work—or rather, to play. There was nothing labored about her efforts.

I had taught myself to please myself and always imagined I was good at it. In truth, I had been an undemanding tutor and lazy pupil in the school of self-pleasure. My strokes had never been more than serviceable. I had never needed more, nor imagined what more there could be.

Lady Bertilak was determined to teach me better.

After she had taken the weight and measure of my cock, she did not hold it in her grip, but ran a single nail up the length of it, underneath. Her finger caught on the ridge below my cockhead, and she tickled it. I blushed. Such delicate attention!

I felt the strangest echoes of the embarrassment I had felt when I had not been able to master my arousal the day before. Now, I was not hurrying down a corridor doubled over because I could not keep my cock from springing out of my drawers. I was in a private chamber, with a lady who had made her intentions clear. Why should her attention have the power to humiliate me so? Why did the blood rushing to my cheeks do nothing to diminish the surge through my cock?

She circled her fingertip around. She tickled, she teased, she pinched. She giggled. She took what I had been taught was the pride of my manhood and made of it an adorable little plaything for herself, and I loved every unbearable moment of it with every unworthy fiber of my being. I bit my lip to keep from crying out at the smallest motion of her fingernail across my skin. She made me gasp even when she refused to touch it, reached out and then refrained with a look that said she was weighing whether it would be worth it.

Even when she began to move her attentions up and down the shaft in the unmistakable rhythm of two bodies coming together, she varied her touches, sometimes gripping tight but more often brushing lightly.

She had masterful fingers, to play such a beautiful tune on a borrowed instrument as to make an amateur of its owner. The word "please" came to my lips again and again, the world's shortest and most heartfelt litany of prayer. I would have begged her in full for release, but life had not yet endowed me with the vocabulary to do so. I expected to burst at any moment, but always she drove me right up to the brink of the cliff and then turned aside. I would have believed my balls would explode, for it seemed impossible she would allow my cock to do so, yet inevitable that something must give if she did not relent.

Then she did.

I came into it with all my body, all my being, behind it. The climax she wrested from me emptied me out, leaving me gutted and hollow, and hung up to dry.

I collapsed, my knees jelly and water, my breath ragged and hard. She left me there on the floor, alongside the mess we had made together.

I thought of running, of fleeing the castle in search of the green chapel, where I could camp for the remaining nights before my fatal appointment.

It was not that I did not wish to play my next part in the game with Lord Bertilak, it was that I was not sure that I could. He had borne the kiss with good grace and more, but surely there had to be limits to hospitality and holiday humor, even in this strange place.

But I could no more have run from Lord Bertilak than I could have turned my back on my pledge to the green knight. I did not wait to be summoned, but went down to meet him a bit before the hour in which he had returned the previous day.

He came back with two retainers carrying the biggest boar I had ever seen, slung on a pole between them.

"Well!" he said. "What do you make of that, Sir Gawain?"

"Joints and chops," I said. "I'd say sausage, but I suspect we could put him to a more immediate use for the night's feast."

"With your kind permission, sir knight!" he said.

"Granted, good lord!" I said.

"And what do you have for me in return?" he said. "I dare say you won't top your offering of yesterday."

"I dare say I will," I said, trying with coy humor to turn aside the rising heat before my head burst with it, "if you are certain you desire it."

"What? Would you have me refuse, only so you can say later that I won our contest by deceit?" he said. "Our terms are clear. The boar is yours, but whatever was given to you during the day is mine."

"Very well, my Lord Bertilak," I said. "You asked for it."

And I gave it to him, beginning with the kiss. The second kiss I gave the man in as many nights was surprisingly comfortable. It was firm and warm, no mere peck on the lips, though it lacked the ardent intensity of the night before, as I feared losing my head, losing myself in the passion of it all and neglecting the true gift I had to give him.

I still was pleased to summon the thought of myself as the

proxy passed between Lady Bertilak and Lord Bertilak. It came to me unbidden, and I doubt I could have chased it away if I had wanted, which I did not.

But I had no pretense this time of making myself into Lord Bertilak's lady wife. I could not have acted with quite the same skill as she did. I had never in my life before that taken hand to cock for any other purpose than immediate relief, and rarely had I touched one not my own for any but the most fleeting and furtive of purposes.

I simply did what came naturally when my hand closed around a hot, thick, meaty cock, smelling of the exertions of the hunt. My hand slipped up and down the shaft. He let out a groan that I was not sure was fully one of pleasure, so I loosened my grip a bit. His callused hand closed itself around mine, showing me the error I had made. Firmer, he wanted, not looser.

I tried to show a measure of the restraint Lady Bertilak had shown me, but then I remembered how it had felt when she had flicked her nail at the ridge where my cock head joined the shaft. As clumsy as my imitation was, he came almost at once.

There was nothing I could do to stop that, but I knew I had not delivered to him everything that he was entitled to, so I continued my ministrations, coaxing his cock back to life. My bewildered host did not seem to know whether to laugh or cry.

"Sir Gawain, you are insatiable," he said.

"My lord, you are," I said. "You did insist on everything you were due."

"I did!" he said, throwing back his head and roaring with laughter.

When I had him sufficiently aroused a second time, I tried even less to imitate exactly the moment-by-moment movements of Lady Bertilak, but rather the joy she had evidently felt in them. For all that he was older, Lord Bertilak was vital and virile, and his cock was a monster equal to the prize he'd given me. It was hot and hard in my hand. The shaft was slick with the glistening remnants of my first fumbling attempt.

Having brought him off once, it was easier to find the edge without pulling him over, and now I could truly give him what I had been given myself, and I did.

I found myself wanting to go further. I could fault the lady little for having left me as she did. She owed me nothing; less than she had given me. But I did not want my lord host to spill his seed upon the floor and then be abandoned. I wanted to take it. I wanted to feel it on my face, I wanted to take it into me, feel it filling my mouth like hot grease from a roast pig. Would I feel it slide down my throat and settle in my stomach like a warm belt of spirits in the winter? What would it make me, to be a man who swallows another man's seed? If the other man was one such as Lord Bertilak, I was sure there would be no shame in it.

Or if there was, the shame would not be of an unpleasant variety. I felt I could drown in that sort of shame and expire with a smile of satisfaction on my face.

Somehow, though, I knew that would be going too far. I could not pretend to stand as proxy for Lady Bertilak while exceeding the boundaries of what I had been handed. I wanted so desperately to take his seed into my mouth, to clean his cock with my lips and tongue, but what pleasure he would gain from this base display, I could not say, and to take as I gave would go against the nature of our contest, which was generosity.

"You are indeed good in giving," he said when I had finished.

"I give, my lord, only as good as I get," I said, and again, the company laughed, lady and lord along with them.

I passed another night between lady and lord, enjoying the company of both with many helpings of roast pork.

The next day, Lord Bertilak rode out again. I doubted little that he would return with some sumptuous gift for me, and less that Lady Bertilak would deliver to my room something that I could give to him.

I wondered what this was, to them. I had no doubt that the lady had spoken truly about their arrangements, that she was within her rights to dally with whom she pleased, which meant that by their reckoning I was within my rights to take what she offered.

Yet it still must be possible for the relations between them to become strained, or for me to overstep my bounds. Perhaps it would have been best if everything had been laid out in the open and discussed beforehand, but having become enmeshed in these games, it seemed too late to sort them out now.

I made up my mind that if somehow I survived my appointment with the green knight, then I would return to Castle Bertilak to clear the air and make such amends as were necessary and possible. In the meantime, I would accept nothing more from the Lady Bertilak and let her husband be declared the winner at the end of the day, the last day of our contest.

"You leave us tomorrow," she said instead of knocking.

She was wearing a gown woven of gold and green thread, her waist wound with a rope girdle of gold and green strands. She was a vision, even with the grief writ over her face. I knew I must give her cheer, however I could.

"Yes, though it might be that my business in the chapel will be concluded in such a way that allows me to return this way," I said. "With no pressing business elsewhere, I could perhaps pass the winter here and travel south when the roads clear."

"Perhaps," she said. "But you deem it unlikely."

"True."

"You believe you will not see me again, after tomorrow."

"Also true," I admitted.

"Then you must take my ring, as a token of remembrance," she said, pulling a twisted gold band set with emeralds off her finger.

"Nay, lady, I could not," I said. "For by rights it would belong to your husband, and anyway, if I cannot return to you, I would not remember you for long, and your fine ring would be lost on the forest floor if it were not carried away by my killer."

"Then take my girdle," she said, untying it and unwinding it from about her waist.

"The problems, my lady, remain."

"Do not be so quick, good Gawain," she said. "What I offer you is magic. This girdle, while I wear it, protects me from harm. It may do the same for you."

"So I would win my contest with the knight through sorcery," I said.

"Be not hasty!" she said. "Do you think he survived beheading through wits or courage?"

She had a point. For the first time since the knight had taken his head back from me, I thought I saw a way forward, a way out. And though I had no right to keep the wondrous gift she offered me, in a moment that I can only see as one of great weakness and shame I made myself believe that this was heaven's design.

"Very well," I said. "But that is all I will accept from you today."

"Then my husband will be suspicious, when you suddenly have no gift for him," she said, and she slid her gown to the floor. "You must give him something of such overwhelming generosity, surpassing all gifts of the past two days, or he will suspect something."

I saw the truth in her words because I wanted so much for them to be true.

I have heard men attempt to describe a lady's bare body often, but rarely in a way that does credit to either the witness or the vision. I shall say that she was lovely in ways that surpass the telling of men. She was lovely with the sturdy weight of her presence, lovely in her years. Her face was warm and hungry, her figure soft and full. Her breasts hung in such a way that you knew they were there in their own right, that they would exist just the same whether any man looked upon them or not.

I fear many young men have been ruined for women by having their heads filled with bawdy tales full of impossible proportions and implausible assignations. For my part, such tales are now spoiled for me. Neat symmetry may be pleasing in a story, but how could I ever stir myself to action over a fantasy figment when I have seen a woman such as Lady Bertilak in the flesh?

You may put your hand to a childish fancy, but you cannot put your cock to it. More men should think on that, before scorning living women in favor of their ideals.

Lady Bertilak went to the bed and bent herself over it, her bare ass offered to me. What else could I have done, except what I did? That was to take her, to take what she was offering. I don't remember pulling out my cock. I don't remember a moment when it became hard, only the sudden awareness that it was.

I do remember going to her, putting my hands on her hips, positioning myself, and then thrusting in.

Unlearned as I am in the arts of love, I know that any lady is owed more preparation than that. All I can say in my defense is that I was not thinking. Heaven be praised, she did not suffer much from my lack of courtesy and foresight. I do not know what tender ministrations she applied to herself before she came to my chamber, but I have never known anyone to be as wet, as warm, or as willing as I found her.

I was on top and she was bent over, but I could not say that I mastered her in any way in that coupling. She met my thrust each time. The writhing of her body beneath mine set the pace and tempo. I played only the tune that she called, danced to the song that she piped. I did not take her, I swear, so much as she took me into her, again and again and again.

Though I came to her full of desperate yearning, still she denied me release until it pleased her. She rode back onto my cock as slowly as suited her, prolonging the encounter until she came shuddering and screaming, once, and then twice, and then a third time, and then, oh, only then did she draw me in deep and hard, clenching tight around me until she wrenched from me my own sweet release.

And then it was done... we were done.

And it hit me.

"How will I ever...?"

"Only offer, sweet Sir Gawain," she said with a laugh. "My husband will know what to make of your gift."

Maybe he would, but I had no idea. I could strip down and bend over the table as she had the bed, but other than having a fine laugh about it, I didn't see how this would benefit Lord Bertilak.

I am sure you are less naive a man than this poor knight was, and certainly Lord Bertilak was wiser than I. He was also more of a gentleman than I had been, a fact for which I must be grateful. But I am getting ahead of myself.

I did, of course, acquit myself as honorably as I could under the circumstances. As Lady Bertilak had stripped herself down, so did I disrobe completely in front of my hosts and their people. As she had flung herself across the bed, I did fling myself against the table, oddly close to my accustomed place at it. As she had lifted her pert buttocks and offered them up to me, spreading her legs slightly so that they might part, I did the same, or I tried to.

This time it was Lord Bertilak who hesitated.

"Are you sure about this, Gawain?" he asked.

"If you are not interested in my generosity, you can declare me the winner," I said. I'd play my role to the hilt, or not at all.

"Aye?" he said. "But on the subject of shared generosity, three times before you have shared my gifts for you with the hall. What if I were to do the same?"

This almost stopped me short, but again, I was committed. I would give it my full measure, or none.

"My lord, this gift is yours to do with as you please," I said.

"Ah, well, as it happens, what I caught for you today won't make for as fine a feast as my other gifts," he said, and it wasn't until this moment that it even occurred to me that in my haste to be seen making good on my half of the bargain, I hadn't waited for him to present his gift for the day. "As the spoils of my hunt will belong to you, so will I take the spoils of your day for myself."

And he did, though not without some gentle preparations.

I should have known before that I was not the first man to kiss Lord Bertilak in fulsome passion upon the lips. I certainly had no doubt after that night that I was not the first man to offer myself to him thusly. He spread my cheeks with his hand and with first one finger and then two, he applied some sort of warm unguent first to the outside of my poor, virginal hole, and then to the inside.

It was... not unpleasant, to my surprise. The feeling of strong fingers brushing down my crack until they found the hole is one that always makes me shiver to recollect, no matter how many times I call it to mind. The pleasure I felt when he first pushed against it was not something I had expected. The pain when he first pushed inward was less than I had imagined, and the pleasure only grew as I felt his fingers sliding in, turning and bending as he sought to widen the way. I found myself unaccountably thinking of Lady Bertilak crooking her finger under my cock to tickle it. Such a similar motion, such different contexts. Again I felt like, in some strange way, husband and wife had made me into their go-between, my whole body a point of contact between them. It sounds unnatural, to hear it said plainly, but it felt so right.

I might have whimpered a bit when he pulled his fingers free, but then his cock, the head of that thick, throbbing instrument that I had held in my hand, was between my cheeks, lined up against the hole. He pushed, and despite all his preparations, I felt the most impossible stretching sensation as he made his slow way in.

The slowness made the pain bearable, though the slowness itself was torture. My host, it seemed, was also determined to play his part to the hilt. He worked his way in until there was nowhere further to go, and that's when he really began to work.

It felt strange, but it also felt good. It was so unlike anything I had felt before, and I wondered if this was anything like Lady Bertilak had felt when I had been in her. Or were the holes so different? But then I thought the most impudent thought that had ever crossed my mind, and this was that Lady Bertilak most certainly had an ass, and this meant she had an asshole of her own. We were in this respect alike, and what could be done to mine, might be done to hers.

Though the physical mechanics of the act might have mirrored each other, I don't believe there was that much in common between her former position and mine. Beneath me, she had fucked me. Before her husband, I was being fucked. In the space of one short day, I found myself mastered by both mistress and master of Castle Bertilak.

The reins were not in my hands, but we still followed a course much like the one his wife had steered. He pounded with steady, sure thrusts in and out. Each time he slammed his way home, it was like a jolt of pure hot pleasure was shoved right through me. That peculiar shivery, delightful feeling of lightness that I had thought came only at the very moment of climax was there with each thrust, as his pounding cock found a point within me that had never been touched before and battered it like a ram.

It was a deep-in-the-bone pleasure, the way a wound may leave a deep pain. It suffused me, grew within me until I thought it would have to burst forth from every part of me, an orgiastic release of body and spirit. Lady Bertilak had teased me to such a point through her restraint, but Lord Bertilak drove me to it with relentless ardor.

Would I be given release? Could there be release? I did not know. This was strange territory for me. My world shrank until it was nothing but the monstrous cock running through me. All thoughts thundered out of my brain except one, which escaped my lips as a whispered prayer: *"Please, please, please...."*

I would swear that neither my hand nor his touched my cock, but it thrashed beneath us like it had a will of its own until I came with a whole-body shudder. My fancy that I might expel my very soul didn't seem like half an exaggeration, but Lord Bertilak had not yet found his own release in me.

He did not stop. I could barely stand it, but I wouldn't for anything in the world have stopped it, certainly not before he had been given the full measure of his pleasure. Whatever had emptied out of me was replaced with his hunger. I wanted him in me, deeper and faster and harder. I was not sure there was any deeper to go, but still I wanted it.

I never got less than half-hard, and it wasn't long before I came again, explosions of light dancing behind my eyes as he hit this certain spot on each thrust. I felt certain I could not take any more of it, that I would die of pleasure commingled with pain, and then I came a third time. I don't even know that anything came out except a gasp, but I felt it all the same.

Then, mercifully, I felt him coming, too. He drove himself as deep into me as he could and then further, straining his hip against my buttocks like he would break me in half. Grunting like a wild man of the north swinging an axe, he buried his seed deep inside me.

The feeling of him pulling himself free of me was the most bittersweet pleasure I've ever received. The cheer that went up when he pushed back from me and put his cock away was louder than any I've ever heard, save one. The memory of the day exactly one year before brought me back to myself in a hurry. I tried to dress, but someone had cleared away my clothes, and so I sat on my stool between my hosts, naked and eating from plates set where I had lain beneath Lord Bertilak until it was time for me to retire.

No one mentioned that I had been rutted by the lord of the strange house on the very table at which we dined, but I could not help but be constantly conscious of the fact. My ass could not forget the uses it had been put to so quickly. My cock would not be roused for anything after such exertions, but it would not lie still. My cheeks were hot, but I could no longer think of what I felt as shame.

The next day, I wordlessly prepared myself for what I was thinking of as my final journey. I had the lady's gift wound about my chest, under my clothes, but despite the fantastic and impossible things I had seen in my life, I had little faith in its ability to protect me.

The knight all in green was real enough, I knew. I had seen what he could do. The wondrous properties of the belt were just a story.

My horse was saddled, and I mounted up alongside Lord Bertilak, who had promised to guide me.

"You have the axe?" he asked, and I nodded.

It was covered in a cloth and strapped to my back.

"So, who won the contest?" I asked. It seemed a feeble jest, but I needed to say something.

"Well, I feel very satisfied with all you have given," he said. "But I have one more gift for you. I should have given it to you yesterday, but you were so eager."

So saying, he handed me a parcel. I unwrapped it to find a fine white fox fur.

"Thank you," I said.

"I told you it wouldn't make much of a feast," he said.

"I'll treasure it," I said. I didn't add *for the rest of my life*, as that might sound bitter. In that moment, I almost came clean about the gift. I wish that I would have. I don't think it would have made a difference either way, but he deserved it.

The ride was short, too short. In no time at all we had arrived at what could only be the green chapel. It was a bower of trees, and they were ever-green. I do not mean to say that they were all pine, but that even in the depths of winter, all of the trees were green. They were spaced so that two men could ride abreast on horses into their midst and stand in a clearing that was utterly free of the snow that covered the land outside.

We dismounted and tied up our horses at the edge.

"So, this is the green chapel," I said. "I'm here. I hope I don't have to wait too long for the green knight. Will you wait with me?"

"There is no need," Lord Bertilak said. "He is here. Give over the axe, and we will be done with it."

I looked at him, and though I had not expected this, I could not find it in me to be surprised. I unwrapped the axe and offered it to him, handle first. As his hand clenched it, a transforming power seemed to surge through his body. His face and limbs grew younger, though his eyes retained the look of youth. His winter clothing fell away, undone and pushed aside by the tendrils that grew around his body. He stood tall, naked, and proud, my knight all in green.

"My lord, I've been looking for you," I said.

"And you have found me, Gawain," he said. "Will you do as you promised?"

I nodded.

"From your lips," he said.

"I will," I said. I kneeled before him. As I had attempted to emulate his lady wife, I did now my best imitation of him, a year and a day before. I took up the same pose, and stuck out my neck. "Strike true."

"Aye, I will," he said softly, and he lifted the axe.

"Wait!" I cried as he started to swing.

"Cowardice, at this late hour? That is most disappointing," he said.

"I am not a coward, or perhaps I have been," I said, getting to my feet. I reached beneath my cloak and tunic and removed the girdle wound about there. "I cannot break both my vows to you, my lord... I was given this yesterday and did not give it forward."

"It's a very pretty cord," he said. "I can understand why you would wish to have a token of my lady-wife, whose company has been such a comfort to you. I would have given it back to you today, if it would have brought you comfort now. But you said both your vows."

"Yes," I said. "For this is why I could not bear to risk giving it up. I sought to defeat your challenge with sorcery, my lord."

"Sorcery?"

"Lady Bertilak told me that her girdle would protect me from harm," I said.

"You may tell her that it worked," he said, and he handed it back to me.

"What, my lord?" I said.

"I said, tell her that it worked," he said.

"But my oath...."

"Is satisfied," he said. "You were willing to take the blow, Gawain. That was the deal I offered, and you more than made good on it. You could have remained in the south. You could have given up your search. You could have fled the castle at any point. You could have accepted the supposed magical protection of my lady's belt. You did none of these things, Gawain, but you gave yourself over, willing and honest."

"And that's all it takes?"

"Have you learned nothing from your time with us?" he chided. "Will is all it ever takes."

Once more, I stood reprieved.

And then I knelt.

"What is this?" Lord Bertilak asked.

"It is my will that you have my head," I said.

"You're certain?"

"You may have it, my lord, from my lips," I said.

His verdant guise offered no enhancement to his cock, but it needed none. The penis stirring from being the greenery was the same I'd so eagerly handled before, the same that had ruled my ass the past night. It did not require any further encouragement than the sight of my willing and parted lips. Setting the axe aside, Lord Bertilak, my knight in green, took hold of my head by both sides, and claimed his proffered prize.

The phrase "to bite off more than one can chew" might apply here in nearly every particular but one, and the one was a near thing; his cock left little room for teeth. As jaws lack the apparently endless elasticity of a man's nethers, the exertions were left to me, and though I had little experience, I had much enthusiasm.

I sucked. I gobbled. I drank in the smell of sweat and man and wood, and luxuriated in it all. My hands addressed what my mouth could not take in. I had wanted this for days. It seemed I had wanted it my whole life long, without knowing it.

I worshipped my knight, my lord, in that green chapel. He answered a year of prayers with a communion as sacred and salty as tears, and I drank down every drop.

That is how I came to be returned living to you from the quest we thought for certain would be my last. With your leave, my king, my return will be brief. The Bertilaks have extended to me the most wonderful offer, and if you will allow me to serve my vow to you while sharing new vows with them, I would fain represent your interests in the northlands, in the wild woods of Caledon and beyond.

They are willing, and if you are also, then so am I.

That's all it ever takes.

The Shape of Camelot Today
Michael M. Jones

The date went well. So well that I let my guard down and let Gwen walk me home. Maybe it was the drinks we'd had over a long, lingering dinner or the spark of chemistry that leapt between us when we both reached for the check at the same time and our hands touched, but I felt the walls of restraint crumble within me. On the walk back to my apartment, we kept bumping into one another, arms brushing, skin tingling. As we made our way up two flights of stairs, I felt her staring at my ass, so I made sure to put some extra swish into my step. And when we reached the right floor, I stopped so suddenly she crashed into me, and we both knew what was going on between us.

By the time we were in front of my door, we were all over one another. She had me pressed up against the wall in a hungry embrace, and we were kissing like we'd both just discovered girls for the first time all over again, and I dropped my keys so I could run my hands through her hair, and her hands were wandering into dangerous territory, and I couldn't catch my breath with her tongue down my throat, and I was so fucking wet and—

I was seconds away from throwing caution to the wind and inviting her inside when a tiny voice of reason intruded. This wasn't the "You barely know her" voice and it definitely wasn't the "You don't do one night stands" voice, because those were both on the sidelines urging me to go for the goal. No, this was the "How the hell do I explain the Sword to her?" voice, and it was like a splash of cold water directly to an overheated libido. Steam everywhere, but I found the mental wherewithal to gently disengage. Chest heaving, cheeks flaming, lips swollen, nipples hard as diamonds—I couldn't have denied my desire or my need for a seriously intense fuck if you'd held a gun to my head. I bent down to retrieve my keys while I mumbled something about an early morning and I couldn't, not tonight.

I met her eyes, a deep chestnut brown, as I straightened up, and recognized that mix of disappointment, embarrassment, and hurt. She thought something had gone wrong, that I was blowing her off. That she'd gone too far and scared me. I placed a hand on her cheek and drew her in for a soft, lingering kiss. "I'll make it up to you," I promised. That seemed to draw some of the sting out of our aborted tryst, and she nodded. I watched as she turned and made her way down the hallway, and it was my turn to admire her ass, tight and muscular from the three miles she said she ran every morning. I thought briefly about taking up running. No, that sounded too much like work. I'd watch her run, though. Bring her water or something.

I ducked into my apartment before she could catch me staring and slumped against the door once it was closed, my eyes shut to better drink in one last image of Gwen Terry, the woman who would most definitely rock my world if I let her. Short and stocky where I was tall and willowy, curvy where I was lean, dark where I was fair; she was my opposite in so many ways. Brown eyes, a mass of dark curls, stubborn features, she reminded me of an oak tree—solid and dependable. But her core was fire, through and through, and I'd felt her blaze to life against me.

"Fire and earth," I murmured. "A dangerous combination." I was all air and water, my long blonde hair, blue eyes, and pale features often called eye-catching if not beautiful. Together, the two of us could work miracles. "She's the one," I said, louder, as I opened my eyes.

The sword in the stone had nothing to say, though it pulsed with an ancient crankiness, its disapproval sweeping against me in something sensed rather than felt. It was truly an old thing, bearing the wear and tear of a weapon used for fighting and killing over many years. Much of its length remained buried in the sizable boulder that took up too much of my living room (acting as the world's weirdest and worst coffee table) but enough protruded to suggest a larger-than-life item created for a larger-than-life individual. The handle was wrapped in dark, cracked leather worn thin by use, and a scarlet gem decorated the pommel. Sometimes, I swore I could see a face within that gem, brought to life when the light was just so.

"Don't give me that," I said in reaction to the Sword's unspoken comment. "If you met Gwen, you'd see it. She's smart, funny, beautiful, a hell of a kisser, and she understands politics." I shook my head and walked past the Sword, heading for my bedroom, which lay at the end of the apartment's short hallway. I dropped my clutch purse on an end table and left a trail of clothes as I stripped along the way. There was something to be said about dressing up for a date, but it was a relief to shed the thigh-length skirt, the not-quite-too-tight blouse, the matching lace bra and panties—Gwen had been so very close to discovering those for herself tonight—and black kitten heels. Oh yes, I'd aimed to leave an impression, and it had succeeded, given the way we'd been pawing each other by the time I cut things short.

I re-emerged from my bedroom after changing into comfy shorts and a loose white tank top and collected my discarded clothes on the way back to the living room, dropping them into the laundry hamper. As though we'd put a conversation on hold, I flopped down on the couch so I could stretch out while still facing the Sword. "I know she's a woman. I know you want me to find some strapping young leader-in-the-making to become your new Arthur, but it's not happening." I gave the Sword my most winning smile. "I told you when this all began that if you left it to me, we'd do things my way."

The Sword redoubled its disapproval, giving me its best attempt at a frown, but I'd grown accustomed to its attitude, to its sulks and moods. Its opinions were quite literally set in stone, and we'd had months to get used to one another.

An image filled my mind: a square-jawed hero, barrel-chested and muscular, radiant and glorious and idealized. A leader of men who could rally the heroes and knights and kings to his cause. A champion of justice, honor, chivalry. A defender of virtue and protector of the weak. He held the Sword aloft, and the wicked fell at his feet.

I snorted. "You've been watching the wrong sort of movies. I'll stop leaving the television on for you if this is the best you can do." I forced the image from my mind with something much more my speed: Gwen as she'd looked in the hallway, lips swollen from kisses, cheeks flushed, clothes rumpled. Oh, yes. Just thinking of her reminded me that I'd gotten all hot and bothered without any satisfaction.

The Sword tried again, thrusting a new memory at me. It was the moment when it had appeared in my living room, amidst a dazzling display of light and melody, crushing a footstool, the old coffee table, and my favorite pair of sandals. Again I saw myself thrown back in surprise. Again I saw myself attempting to draw the Sword from the stone in curiosity—wouldn't you?—only to be overcome by a flood of information.

When my fingers wrapped around the ancient hilt that first time, lightning ripped through my body, setting my mind ablaze with a torrent of images. Dozens of lives, of other incarnations. All the Camelots that ever had been or almost were. So much glory and ambition, so much grief and tragedy. And at the center of it all was the Lady of the Lake. She who raised Lancelot, who bestowed Excalibur upon King Arthur, who enchanted Merlin.

Nimue.

Viviane.

Nyneve.

Elaine.

The names and roles were endless, conflicting, and overwhelming. I woke up hours later with a raging headache and a sense of purpose. Excalibur wanted me to find a new King Arthur, so we might start things all over again.

And I'd naturally balked at the whole thing. Because in that cascade of past lives and long-gone cycles, I'd realized something.

it rarely ended well for those involved. Love triangles shattered friendships and destroyed kingdoms. Camelot fell every time, and took with it the light and glory of the age. Lovers were parted by honor or foolish mistakes or misunderstandings. Chivalry led to tragedy.

I swore that if I was to play Lady of the Lake and bestow the Sword upon some worthy person, it would be my choice... and we'd seen enough Arthurs. It was time for a Guinevere to have a chance to shine. I'd spent a year looking for a worthy candidate, but every single time, the Sword had rejected them, repulsing them with scorn and dismissal.

Luckily, it was also capable of blurring the memories of those it rejected. Instead of being known as the woman with the freaky sword in her living room, I was just the one with the really awful roommate, and there was never another date after that.

But Gwen was the one, and I could feel it.

Speaking of Gwen... I slipped my hand into my shorts, gasping a little as my fingers grazed against sensitive skin and the lingering heat of arousal. I closed my eyes so I could focus on thoughts of her, and felt the Sword withdraw in frustration.

Yes, I'd discovered a perverse exhibitionist streak that came out to play in front of my inanimate gatecrasher. I slowly teased myself, drawing forth the pleasure, spreading my lips and stroking my clit. I imagined what Gwen might look like between my legs, putting that silver tongue to good use, and my hips arched in unconscious response. "Fuck," I whimpered. My fingers moved quicker as I altered between rubbing my clit and sliding them into an increasingly damp pussy. My breathing grew ragged, and the orgasm was quick in coming tonight, fueled by my lust for Gwen.

Afterward, I lay languidly on the couch, too satisfied to move. The Sword sighed, put-upon but begrudgingly tolerant of my antics. I felt it withdraw as it went to "sleep," entering a state of dormancy where, I figured, it dreamed of a time when men were mighty and women behaved themselves. And why didn't it do that sooner, before I had my way with myself? I guess it liked to watch....

I got up, heading to the bathroom to clean up before going to bed myself. The Sword was a strange thing, I mused. I'd done a lot of research into the Celtic myths after it arrived and dumped its load of knowledge into my head, and so much of it was multi-layered and contradictory, elements drawn from different traditions, different countries, different authors. It was hard to tell where things truly began or what was real. According to the Sword, it was all real, if you bought into the idea of mythic cycles. It made my brain hurt.

It also seemed to be shaped by popular belief, which is how I'd ended up with something out of myth, half-real and half-fictionalized, instead of a true thing. A sword that hewed to a pop-culture interpretation of stories written centuries ago by long-gone people.

The real problem was that you couldn't just go to an Arthurian scholar and tell them about a magical sword in a stone in your living room.

I fell asleep still mulling over the situation. My dreams were filled with fire and shadow, ravens and rivers, castles and knights... and, of course, Gwen. When I woke up, I knew I had to see her again.

"I really am sorry about last night," I said.

"Stop apologizing," Gwen said with a laugh, reaching out to pat my hand. "I understand, really. I... I'm not sure what came over me either. I'm not usually so...."

"Aggressive? Voracious? Mind-blowing?" I suggested, taking comfort in her easy manner and the warmth of her touch. I'd texted her when I woke up, and now here we were, enjoying a round or three at The Velvet Trap, Puxhill's favorite destination for dykes and drinks. (Seriously, that was their motto.) It was weird: it was like my world had been black and white all day, but as soon as I saw her, everything blazed with new life. In her tan-and-cream suit, she looked amazingly dapper, while I felt like an innocent schoolgirl all over again. Not that I'd ever been *that* innocent....

"Mind-blowing? Really?" Gwen ducked her head as if to hide a blush. "I was in a daze the whole way home. I dreamed of you, you know."

"Good dreams?" I asked.

She paused for a moment, the hesitation just long enough to set me to worrying. "Yes... and weird. I should never have leftover pizza before bed."

I winced. "That's a lesson I learned long ago. Especially if it's pepperoni or Hawaiian."

She shuddered. "You eat pineapple on your pizza? That's unnatural. I don't know if this can work out. I take pizza very seriously."

"I'm willing to negotiate," I replied dryly. I took a sip of my drink to wet my lips before asking, "So you said weird dreams?"

Gwen nodded. "I don't remember much. Just, like, a sword in a stone, and a castle, and a lot of darkness. But you were there, and you gave me the sword and then everything felt right. The darkness receded, and then I woke up." She laughed, shaking her head. "I told you, weird. I must have had *Lord of the Rings* on my mind or something."

Gwen's hand hadn't gone far after she released me. This time, it was I who reached out, and I wrapped both hands around hers, feeling the strength in her fingers and the smoothness of her skin. I thought I even felt her pulse, spiking with the unexpectedly intimate nature of my actions. Whatever she'd been about to say was caught in her throat, and she looked at me, brown eyes deep with questions.

"I know this is moving kind of quick," I said, "but I really like you. And I want to see where things go between us."

She must have seen something in my expression. "But...?"

"There's something we have to do before we go further."

"I've been tested," she said promptly, "and I'm clean."

That got a laugh from me. "Oh! Yes, well, that's good to know. Great, really. That wasn't what was on my mind though. I... well, you have to come back to my place and meet my roommate."

"I thought you said you lived alone?"

I shrugged a little. "It's complicated."

Now she frowned. "I don't like the sound of 'complicated.' If that's your thing, fine, but I'm a serial monogamist—one woman at a time."

I rubbed my temples to ward off the oncoming headache. This was coming out all wrong. "No, it's not like that, honest." I sighed. "It's just that there's someone in my life who gets a say in who I date, and while I'm pretty sure they'll approve of you, it's still a thing that has to be done."

Her brow furrowed. "So I have to meet your cat? Cats? Are you warning me that you're a dyke with too many cats? Because I'm okay with anything up to four. After that, I feel outnumbered for real."

I laughed again. "I wish. Can you humor me on this? Please?"

Gwen thought about it for a moment before shrugging. "Sure. But only because you're a hell of a kisser," she allowed. She finished off the rest of her drink before standing. "Okay, let's do this."

"Now?"

"Is there a better time?"

I had to admit that there wasn't.

My steps slowed the closer we got to my apartment building. I forced myself to breathe evenly, but the nervousness had crept in, leaving me unsure about my decision after all. Was I doing the right thing? Was I moving too fast? Would Gwen end up like the others, with fuzzy memories and no desire to be with me?

Gwen's fingers laced with mine, granting me her strength and warmth. "I feel like I'm going to meet the parents. Just like prom all over again."

"You went to prom? Guy or girl?" I asked.

She sighed. "Guy. Best friend. I was still in a lot of denial at the time. Somehow we thought we could hammer a perfectly good friendship into a different shape, and ended up breaking the whole thing into jagged pieces."

I squeezed her hand in reassurance. "I didn't even go. I knew who and what I wanted, and if I couldn't have it, there was no point in pretending. My school didn't even get a Rainbow Alliance until several years after I graduated." Somehow, talking about this calmed me, and before I knew it, we were once again at my door, with Gwen pleasantly close behind me. I unlocked the door and stepped aside. "Please, enter."

She did. She took several steps before stopping dead in her tracks to stare at my bizarre centerpiece. "You have a sword. In a stone. In your living room. And it is huge," she noted. "Lana, that is amazingly geeky. Is it some sort of art piece? Or are you the world's most enthusiastic Arthurian nerd?"

I smiled ruefully and joined her, having shut the door behind us. "Yes, no, maybe. This is my roommate."

"Your roommate is a sword? I'm not tracking you." Gwen pulled her attention away from the Sword to give me a confused look, nervousness mixed in. I saw the way her body tensed as she reassessed her safety with me. There was geeky, and there was weird.

"What if I said that in order to date me, you have to draw the sword from the stone?" I offered to defuse things. "She who is worthy, and all that?"

"You do realize you don't need a gimmick to get into my pants," Gwen teased. "I mean, I already find you hot as fuck and was ready to leap into your bed last night. This isn't necessary." She reached out, running a single finger along my cheek, and I shivered, a frisson of delight rippling through me. I gulped.

"It's important to me."

She shook her head indulgently. "I'll play along." She approached the Sword, one slow step at a time. I felt the Sword's presence intensify, judging her in its unique manner. Disapproval, of course—it wanted a man—but a tiny amount of curiosity. If a sword could furrow its brow, this one would. Gwen stretched out a hand. I held my breath. She wrapped her fingers around the handle. Time stood still. The air was dead. All was silent.

She tugged at the sword, and for a moment, nothing. It remained resolute in its stony embrace, and I knew, just knew, that I'd failed yet again.

Then our world exploded. The stone shattered into a million shards of light, each one reflecting back different worlds and times, different versions of Gwen and myself, different Camelots. It was dazzling, overwhelming, blinding. I threw up a hand to shield my eyes, but all I could see were dancing spots. Nearby, far away, somewhere, Gwen screamed in shock and awe—not pain— and a voice roared:

WORTHY
THE CYCLE BEGINS ANEW
CHOOSE

And though winds howled, and the voice deafened us, and we were blinded by the light, still we found one another, hands coming together in a tight clasp.

"What is this?" Gwen yelled over the confusion. "I—the sword is telling me so much, showing me visions—how is this happening?"

There was no way I could put it into words, so instead I drew her close and kissed her fiercely, the Sword trapped between our bodies. The long metal blade was both icy cold and burning hot, but neither so much that we couldn't stand it. Gwen's lips, already open from her yelling, met mine with surprise and then eager welcome. She accepted me as a familiar thing, a rock in the maelstrom, and embraced me as best she could with one hand still gripping the Sword—which seemed to have shrunk to fit her smaller grasp and frame.

And the magic spilling forth all around us granted me the ability to speak to her mind, to wordlessly convey everything I knew, everything the Sword had told me. *You, I told her, can determine the course of the future. You can create the new Camelot, inspire heroes, stand against the dark. You can lead us.* I tried to convey my hopes, that she'd bring something new to the eternal cycle, that she could change a mythology that had already been much changed over the centuries. And I told her that I would be there for her.

The Lady of the Lake to her Arthur.

Lana to her Gwen.

Around us, the chaos paused, hanging in a formless void like a thousand shining stars, as the world waited to see what would happen next. Never before had the Sword been taken up by a woman. Never before had the Lady of the Lake acted so willfully, so directly. Never had Camelot's nature been in such flux.

Gwen broke the kiss and pulled back to meet my gaze. In the new silence, she said breathlessly, "I can't. This is too much."

"You can, or the Sword would never have accepted you."

"I won't know what to do."

"You'll figure it out."

"What if I'm not the right sort of person? What if I screw it up?"

"Be the person you want to be. Make mistakes. Learn from them."

"But—"

I shushed her with a finger to the lips. "Listen to me, Gwen. No one comes to this prepared. No one comes to this perfect. You're only human." The words came from a wisdom buried deep within me, echoing through the centuries. A hundred Ladies of the Lake had reassured a hundred questioning Arthurs, in one way or another.

"But... I can't slay monsters, I'm not like that."

"It's not about killing monsters or slaying dragons or dueling knights," I said. "That was a different era. There are different challenges to overcome. We fight our duels in the courts with words instead of swords, and gather allies through social media." I held her gaze. "You can do this."

"No," Gwen said. "*We* can do this." She grabbed my hand and drew it to join hers around the Sword's hilt. Electricity tore through us, bringing us together, and I saw how the universe worked. I saw the building blocks of creation, the threads of creation—however you want to describe it, I understood the fundamental nature of the story. And together, Gwen and I, we reached out to shape the next Camelot.

We shaped it with caresses and kisses, the Sword seeming to fall away between us as the void shrunk and my apartment, in all its mundanity, returned. We shaped Camelot as our bodies entwined and our passions grew.

Our battles would be for equality, acceptance, and tolerance.

Our knights would be everyday people standing up against the wicked, the selfish, the bigoted, the close-minded, the cowardly, the cruel.

Our victories would come one at a time, hard-fought and long-overdue, with the striking down of old laws and passing of new ones.

Our legacy would be subtle yet lasting, creating a world where you could go to prom with whoever you chose, where you could figure out who you were without fear of rejection or hatred.

And it would all start here, as Gwen and I, back in my living room, broke our embrace, only to stare at each other with wide eyes and heaving chests. And it was she who pushed me back toward the couch, though I fell quite willingly, dragging her down with me so we collapsed together.

I tried to capture her in another kiss, but she was more interested in getting me out of my clothes, so I cooperated. She yanked my blouse over my head and tossed it aside, while I simply tore her shirt open, buttons flying everywhere to reveal lush breasts, dark skin contrasted by a white lace bra. I tugged the cups of the bra down to expose her, desperate to get hands and mouth on already-pebbled nipples. But oh, her wandering hands threatened to distract me, especially as they roamed along my increasingly sensitive skin.

I moaned; she whimpered. I gasped; she murmured nonsense sounds of approval.

More clothes went flying, some of them irreparably damaged by our haste. She shimmied out of her skirt, letting it and her panties puddle on the floor, revealing gorgeous legs and a pussy glistening with arousal, neatly trimmed. Fierce need hit me like a hammer, and this time when I pulled her in for a kiss, she allowed it. Lips parted and tongues danced, and our hands came to rest on hips and waists for several long moments.

She was fire and earth—blazing hot wrapped around an unwavering core of strength. I was air and water—always moving with fluid grace, soaked with desire, never still as I reacted to her touches and caresses. Together, the elements complemented and amplified one another, acting in unison rather than opposition.

She slipped a hand between my legs, finding me wet and writhing. She massaged my pussy with her fingers, rubbing my clit to keep me on the edge. I bit her nipple, trapping it between my teeth, flicking my tongue over it in response. The delighted squeak she made served as encouragement, and I used a free hand to pinch her other nipple at the same time. That got a muffled shriek against my shoulder of "Fuck yes!" She thrust her fingers into me, and I exploded for the first time, the orgasm sweeping outward from cunt to head and toe, my entire body celebrating this moment of release.

Lust and magic fueled us, and as soon as I had a free breath, I seized the opportunity. I was determined to find out how she tasted; I maneuvered her so that suddenly, she was the one on the couch and I was on top, sliding down to kneel between her legs, and when I buried my face in her pussy, it was sweet and glorious. She was so hot, and so wet, and she made such delightful sounds as my tongue lapped at her, and when her hips arched and her fingers tangled in my hair, I knew she'd have no complaints. Not now, not ever.

Gwen came with a long scream of joy as I coaxed forth an orgasm with my tongue against her clit and my fingers fucking her cunt, and when the first subsided, I pushed her to another, and a third still before she begged for mercy. I licked her clean before granting her that mercy, before moving back up to pull her close in an intimate, momentarily satiated embrace.

There we lay, catching our breath, basking in each other's warmth, letting the initial intensity fade.

But we weren't done quite yet. Camelot hovered around us, almost fully realized but needing some final act to lock it into being. We could feel it. I gazed dreamily at Gwen, fingers idly stroking over a breast while she moved a hand along the curve of my hip. "Your Majesty," I teased her softly.

"My Lady of the Lake," she returned. And then her eyes moved past me, to something on the floor nearby. I awkwardly twisted to follow her, and I saw what she had seen:

The stone was long gone. The Sword was gone as well... but it had left something in its place. Or perhaps it had been transmogrified into something better suited to our ideals and temperaments.

It was the Excalibur of dildos. A magnificent thing of glass a foot long, shaped like a sword, though its blade was made for fucking, not fighting, and its hilt—still with a red gem suspended in the pommel—made it able to service two people at once. All the colors of the rainbow sparkled and swirled within, never quite still.

"No," I said, both aghast and fascinated.

"Yes," said Gwen, with a wicked grin. She disentangled herself from me to go and take up the dildo. It fit in her hand perfectly.

It fit in my pussy perfectly.

She proved worthy of wielding it... over and over, until I was wrung out and unable to move.

Camelot—our Camelot—locked into existence with one last chime, though the ripples of its creation would linger for years to come, as we discovered just what we'd wrought. But we were ready for it.

Contributors

Alexandra Erin is a speculative poet, satirist, and self-published author. Her best-known works include the sprawling web serial *Tales of MU*, several satirical riffs on the 2015 Hugo Awards controversies, and a caption she once wrote on someone's picture of Batman and Superman so it looked like Superman was singing the song from Aladdin. Find her on the web at www.alexandraerin.com.

Katya Harris lives in the UK with her family and spends most of her free time writing stories of lust and love. You can find her on Twitter @Katya_Harris and at misskatyaharris.wordpress.com. She hopes you like what she's written and that you'll come back for more.

Michael M. Jones lives in Southwest VA, with too many books, just enough cats, and a wife who is worthier to rule than he is. He is a frequent contributor to Circlet anthologies, including *Like a Mask Removed* and *Fantastic Erotica*, and is the author of *Puxhill by Night: Lesbian Erotic Urban Fantasy*. He is also the editor of *Like Fortune's Fool* and *Like a Cunning Plan*. For more, visit him at www.michaelmjones.com.

Yolande Kleinn may be a shameless dreamer and a stubborn optimist, but she is also a proud purveyor of erotic romance. Excitable, fastidious, and a little eclectic, she spends every spare moment writing the stories she wants to read. These range from the historical to the modern to the downright fantastic, always with plenty of heat along the way. You can find Yolande online via her website, www.yolandekleinn.com.

Jennifer Levine is the Managing Editor of Circlet Press, where she enjoys wrangling other editors into submission (and some authors, too). Other Circlet anthologies she has edited include *Like a God's Kiss*, *Apocalypse Sex*, *Masked Pleasures*, *What Happens at the Tavern Stays at the Tavern*, *Silent Shadows Come*, and *Charming*. In her spare time she writes fantasy novels, cuddles with her husband and dog, and decorates (and eats) far too many cakes.

Charles Payseur currently resides in Wisconsin, where his partner, a gaggle of pets, and more craft beer than is strictly healthy help him through the long winters. His work has appeared or is forthcoming at *Nightmare Magazine*, *Strange Horizons*, and *Lightspeed Magazine's Queer's Destroy Science Fiction*. You can find him around the internet as contributor to a number of sites and on his blog, Quick Sip Reviews (www.quicksipreviews.blogspot.com), as well as on Twitter as @ClowderofTwo.

Jean Roberta teaches English and creative writing at a Canadian university and writes in several genres. Over 100 of her stories have appeared in print anthologies, as well as in four single-author collections, including a set of woman-centered historical stories, a "bawdy novella," and the occasional scholarly article. She contributes to the ten-writer blog "Oh Get a Grip" and the blog of the Erotic Readers and Writers Association. Find more on her Amazon author page and on her website, www.jeanroberta.com.

More titles you may enjoy from Circlet Press!

What Happens In The Tavern Stays In The Tavern
edited by Jennifer Levine
ISBN: 9781613900666

The word "fantasy" evokes many different responses in people, but the epic fantasy quest is the heart of the genre. Heroes and heroines set off to defeat evil. Haven't you ever wondered what happens behind the scenes, during the downtime the authors gloss over? What Happens at the Tavern Stays at the Tavern gives us the peek behind the curtains we've all been waiting for.

Touch of Steel by A.D.R. Forte
ISBN: 9781613901038

Six, brand new, original stories by A.D.R. Forte that weave science-fiction and fantasy with the erotic power of soldiers, hunters, and fighters of all kinds. A captain and his mysterious colonel, a dragon hunter and her wizard companion, and many more all find a temporary peace in the arms of their respective lovers in these seductive tales.

Like A Midsummer Night
edited by Nicola Klaus & Cecilia Tan
ISBN: 9781613900628

Explore the sexy side of Shakespeare with these six seductive tales that follow the Bard's timeless characters into the bedroom and beyond! Spanning times and places from ancient Rome to other planets in the distant future, these stories mix sex, magic, disguises, gender-bending, and tangled relationships into a brew as heady as the juice of any magic flower.

www.ingramcontent.com/pod-product-compliance
Lightning Source LLC
Chambersburg PA
CBHW072003170626
46813CB00005B/1984